MOON BASE

On the surface of the Moon the 'cold war' continues: world powers watch each other and wait . . . After a series of mysterious events, Britain's Moon Base personnel are visited by a Royal Commission. Among them is Felix Larsen, there to secretly probe the possibility of espionage. But he faces many inexplicable incidents . . . What are the strange messages emanating from the Base? Where are they from? And what is the fantastic thing that has been conceived in the research department?

E. C. TUBB

MOON BASE

Complete and Unabridged

LINFORD
Leicester

First published in Great Britain

First Linford Edition
published 2007

British Library CIP Data

Tubb, E. C.
  Moon base.—Large print ed.—
Linford mystery library
1. Lunar bases—Fiction 2. Spy stories
3. Large type books
I. Title
823.9'14 [F]

ISBN 978–1–84617–792–7

Published by
F. A. Thorpe (Publishing)
Anstey, Leicestershire
Set by Words & Graphics Ltd.
Anstey, Leicestershire
Printed and bound in Great Britain by
T. J. International Ltd., Padstow, Cornwall

This book is printed on acid-free paper

1

It was cold in the hangar and Felix wished they would get on with it. His head still drummed from the roar of the retro-rockets and he still ached from the punishing thrust of take-off but, it seemed, you just didn't walk into Luna Station. There were formalities.

First identification. Then the formal request and equally formal permission to enter. The whole thing smacked of navy-type ritual, natural enough, he supposed, but tedious even though the station was a military establishment. But, finally, the inner doors swung open and they stumbled into the base.

Lord Severn, of course, took it all in his stride and Felix felt a sneaking admiration for the old man. No one could tell from his expression of the discomfort he must be in, but the diplomat was used to travel and had long since learned to wear the mask of graciousness in every situation.

'Sir Ian!' His tone was one of pleasure at having met an old friend. 'It's good to see you again. Seven years, isn't it? A long time to be away from home. You know General Watts, of course.'

The general, presenting his usual enigmatic vagueness, clumsily shook hands but his eyes, shadowed beneath the brim of his uniform cap, darted like gimlets over the vestibule. They rested with particular intentness on the file of men who, with rifles at the present, stood in stiff salute. Their stance was impressive but their numbers were not. They would, thought Felix, just about make a reasonable guard of honour at a not too fashionable wedding.

Then it was his turn to be introduced.

'This is Professor Larsen, Sir Ian. He travelled with us.'

'Welcome to the Moon,' smiled Macdonald. His handclasp was firm, his eyes direct. 'I won't ask you how you enjoyed your trip — I know the answer. Those rockets are sheer murder. Odd, when you come to think of it. Our most modern form of transport is the most uncomfortable ever devised. Still, that's the price of progress.'

Felix smiled, liking the man for trying to be polite and wondered how he was going to correct the Director's obviously false impression of the reason for his presence. Lord Severn did it for him.

'This young man's yours, Sir Ian, he isn't with us. Whitehall sent him here and he rode up with the Commission.'

'Commission?'

'Why yes, dear chap, we've come to look you over.'

For a moment Macdonald looked blank and Felix felt a sharp sympathy for the man immediately followed by a quick admiration at his self-control. It was a hell of a way for anyone to learn that he and his establishment were the subject of a Royal Commission of inquiry.

'I'm afraid that I don't understand, Lord Severn.' The Director was sharp. 'Why was I not informed?'

'Political necessity, dear chap, you know how it is.' Severn was bland. 'No need to create a lot of fuss and bother when it isn't essential. It was impossible to inform you of what was planned without telling the world of our intentions.' He coughed. 'You understand, I'm sure. The political situation is . . . ' he made an awkward gesture, ' . . . delicate. It is best to keep a thing like this to ourselves. But there is nothing personal in this, I assure you. Her Majesty's Government holds you in the highest esteem, the very highest esteem, but . . . ' Another gesture and a smile completed the sentence.

'I see.' If Macdonald had intended to pursue the matter he'd changed his mind, but Felix could sense the rage he must be feeling. 'Are these other gentlemen the rest of your party?'

'Yes, come and meet them, they've heard a lot about you.' Severn smiled blandly as he moved awkwardly towards the others. Connor, the accountant. Prentice the biologist. Meeson the junior minister. It was, he joked, a very small team and it would probably work faster than any Royal Commission in history.

Macdonald, from his expression, was not amused.

★　★　★

A little at a loss Felix waited, not knowing quite what to do. Around him, in the fifty-foot square vestibule, the reception committee disintegrated as they resumed normal activity. The file of soldiers dissolved beneath snapped commands, disappearing into one of the tunnels with which the room was pierced. A group of white-coveralled personnel stood talking and some space-suited men, helmets swung back on their shoulders, passed him on the way to the hangar. Finally he lumbered towards a blond, scandinavian-type man standing on his own.

'Steady!' A hand gripped his arm and he looked down into the vivacious features of a girl. Almost immediately he corrected the impression. She was almost his own age which meant that she was past thirty, but her cropped brown hair and smooth skin matched her slim figure. The name lettered over her left breast told him she was Avril Simpson.

'Hello,' she said. 'I'm the dietician and I've been told that you've come to join us.'

'That's right.' Felix held out his hand and almost fell as the gesture spun him round. She laughed at his awkwardness.

'Take it easy, you're not on Earth now. The trick in this gravity is to move in miniature slow-motion. Walk as if you're going to take a six-inch step. Move your arms as if you're dying of fatigue. You'll soon get used to it.'

'And if I don't?'

'Then you'll suffer from strained muscles, torn ligaments and even broken bones. Try walking now, but do it slowly.'

Cautiously he did as she advised. It was an odd feeling, almost as if he had the strength of a giant which, in a way, he had. But it was a dangerous strength.

'That's better.' Slipping an arm through his she led him towards the group who stood, still gossiping. They fell silent as he approached.

'Meet some of the gang,' introduced Avril. 'You can read their names so I won't introduce you. This is Professor Larsen, folks, he hasn't been branded yet.'

'That's the first essential,' said Jeff Carter solemnly. He was a short, swarthy man with a pronounced widow's peak. 'We've enough to remember as it is and every little helps.' He held out his hand. 'Pleased to have you join us, Professor.'

'Call me Felix.'

'The cat that kept on walking, eh?' Jeff grinned. 'Well, you've certainly walked a long way, about as far as you can get, in fact. What's your line?'

'I'm just a mechanic.'

'So?'

'I've come up to install some electronic hardware,' he explained. 'Nothing to do with the present set-up of the station. I've some laser-beam equipment coming up and I'm to fix and install it.'

'Laser-beams?' Bob Howard, the scandinavian-type he had seen before, pursed his lips in a soundless whistle. 'Heat rays, no less. Why, for Pete's sake? Are we expecting an invasion?'

'It's those dirty Reds,' said another

man. 'We've got to be ready on land, on the sea, in the air and now, more than ever, in space. Hell, it makes you sick!'

'Wait until Crombie hears about this,' said Jeff. His eyes were sharp as they stared at Felix. 'How about that? Does he know or is this another little surprise Whitehall is springing on us?'

'Don't ask me.' Felix shook his head. 'I only work here.'

'Imagine them springing a Commission on Sir Ian without a word of warning.' Avril was indignant. 'And that old fool Severn lying his head off about Security. What's the matter with all those penpushers? Have they forgotten how to write?'

'Those laser beams interest me,' broke in Bob. He pressed closer to Felix. 'How do you manage to get the beam phase so that . . . '

'Hold it!' Felix smiled and shook his head. 'I told you, I'm just the mechanic. As far as I know the details are buried deep in red tape.'

'But — '

'Give him a rest, Bob.' Felix breathed a

8

sigh of relief as Avril came to the rescue. 'The poor devil's only just arrived. Why, he hasn't even had a chance to get adjusted and you want him to join you in one of your gab-sessions. Well, I'm not having it.'

'Three cheers for the women,' said a man sourly. 'Trust them to interfere.'

'You'd miss us,' said Avril caustically. 'Anyway, there'll be time for talk later. Now, I guess, he'd like to see something of his new home.'

It was as he'd expected. Gouged from the solid rock at the foot of a mountain, Luna Station was a complex of tunnels, rooms and inclines all lit with lamps which simulated natural sunlight. Many of the corridors were fitted with metal doors hinged on both edges so that they could be opened from either side; an obvious precaution against accident or attack.

'You want to be careful of these,' warned Avril the first time they reached one. 'It could happen that some fool is opening it from one side while you're on the other. Even in this gravity it isn't nice

9

to be smacked in the face with a sheet of metal.'

'Why not a pane of transparent plastic?'

She shrugged. 'Some genius in the War Office never thought of that and it's too late to alter the specifications.'

He nodded and clumsily, but gaining confidence with every step, followed his guide until he was hopelessly lost.

'You'll soon get used to it,' said Avril cheerfully when he complained. 'For the first few days you'll need a guide, be nice and I'll volunteer.'

'Surely you're too busy to spend time on a stranger.'

'I'll fit you in.' She smiled up at him and he smiled back, warming to her nearness. 'Married?'

'Not now.'

'Dead?'

'Divorced.' He felt he had to add to the bald statement. 'We didn't get on,' he explained. 'When that happens it's best to part. We had no children so it wasn't too hard.'

'Parting is always hard,' she said sombrely, then brightened. 'I wouldn't have said that you were hard to get on with. Tall, dark, intelligent eyes and a mouth that isn't a trap. I'd say you've been around quite a bit.'

She was, he realised with inner amusement, trying to flirt with him.

'That's why I left home,' he said seriously. 'I just couldn't beat them off any longer.' Devilishly he added: 'And I've heard that the most beautiful women in the system are to be found on the Moon.'

'Are they?'

'Well . . . ' He looked at her, letting his eyes rove over her coverall with deliberate lechery. 'From the sample I'd be prepared to say they are.'

'You're sweet!' Impulsively she planted a kiss on his mouth. 'Let's get on with the tour.'

They passed recreation rooms, stores, sleeping chambers and gymnasiums. They passed many sealed, enigmatic doors and he pointed to one before which stood an armed guard.

'Where does that lead?'

'To the bug factory.' She pulled at his

arm. 'You won't be going down there.'

There were many places, he realised, where he wouldn't be expected to go, but he would worry about that when the time came. In the meanwhile he listened to the chatter of his guide as she showed him around. They halted as a file of men walked past. They were hot and grimed and had obviously been doing heavy manual labour.

'We're extending all the time,' explained Avril as he stared after them. 'This place is much larger than when I came.'

'When was that?'

'Five years ago. I've served my time.'

'Going back home?'

'No. Surprised? Well, you shouldn't be. I've no one to go home to so I might as well stay where I'm comfortable.'

Comfort, he mused, remembering the seemingly endless borings through the rock and the mine-like atmosphere of the establishment, was relative, but he didn't say so. She must have guessed his thoughts.

'Maybe living like a mole isn't the best way to grow old but it has its compensations. Good company, real companionship and interesting work. We get along. You'll see.'

He nodded, feeling strangely light-headed, the nagging ache which had ridden in his temples since he landed increasing to a throb of real agony. The marching lights were haloed with tiny rainbows and the glare hurt his eyes. When he touched his face he discovered that he was sweating.

'Are you feeling ill?' She had noticed the gesture.

'Just a headache. I'm all right.'

'You don't look it.' She was anxious. 'If you feel queer then say so. Low gravity gets some people that way at first.'

'Stop worrying.' He tried to smile and then, intending to step forward, suddenly found himself pressed hard against the rough stone of the corridor. Desperately he swallowed the saliva filling his mouth.

'You *are* ill!' Her face was very close to his own. 'I'm a fool. I should have had better sense.'

'It's just that I feel a little sick,' he confessed. 'It'll pass.'

'You've overdone it,' she said. 'It's my fault but I just didn't think. Your sense of balance is all to hell and your eyes are fighting your reflexes. I should have known it would happen but you seemed to adapt so well I just didn't think. I'm sorry.'

Her concern seemed genuine but he was feeling too miserable to analyse it.

'How about the others?'

'Severn and his mob? They'll be all right, Sir Ian has better sense than I have. They're probably sitting nice and quietly with Gloria fussing over them to see that they're comfortable.' She gripped his arm. 'What you need is rest and some food. Can you make another two hundred yards to the dining-room? You can crawl if you like. I won't mind.'

Fortunately for his masculine pride he didn't have to crawl.

★ ★ ★

The food was a surprise. He had expected a tiny portion of protein knowing that plentiful calories weren't needed when there was little physical exertion, but his plate was heaped with something like spaghetti covered in a thick, brown sauce.

'Synthetic, of course,' explained Avril. 'Mostly bulk from the chollera vats flavoured with yeast derivitives.' She began to eat her own, smaller meal. 'It takes time to break the habits of a lifetime and to the stomach small quantity means small nourishment. So we design the meals to fool old mother nature. Anyway, we don't want to contract the stomach by disuse more than we have to. So we compromise with a low-calorie diet with plenty of bulk. Eat up, now, and you'll soon feel better.'

Dutifully he forced himself to eat knowing that, if he were to succumb to nausea, it would be better to do so on a full stomach, but it was hard work.

'I'll get some tea.' Avril rose and walked to the serving counter and, while she was gone, a pert brunette accompanied by two men sat at the table. She smiled at Felix.

'Hello, there! Are you the new one?'

Felix nodded.

'Glad to have you with us. Where are you from?'

'London, Maida Vale.'

'You don't say! I'm from Willesden and that makes us almost neighbours. What's the West End like nowadays? Have they finished building the M.1 extension to Finchley yet? Just what did happen in the Hyde Park riots last year? Is it true that . . .'

'Give him a rest, Mary.' Avril had returned and stood glaring at the other woman. 'Can't you see he's suffering from low-g?'

'Sorry, I didn't know.'

'Well, you do now. And you can take those big, cow's eyes off him, he's mine!'

Rudely she shoved the other woman off her place on the bench. Mary resisted and for a moment they struggled in soundless violence. Then one of the men parted them with a grin on his freckled face.

'Take it easy, girls,' he chuckled. 'If you want to fight do it in the gym.' He winked at Felix as if they shared a common bond. Mary hesitated, then reluctantly moved over. Triumphantly Avril sat down and

16

gave Felix his cup.

'Tea,' she said. 'God's gift to the British. What would we do without it?'

'Drink coffee,' snapped Mary. 'Others do.'

'No thanks.' The man who had winked at Felix stared solemnly at the little group. Felix couldn't make out his name. Sipping his tea he tried to conquer the waves of nausea rising from his stomach.

His head swam and he had the horrible conviction that, at any moment, he was going to be sick. The buzzing in his temples was deafening and his whole body streamed with perspiration. Eyes closed against the unbearable brilliance of the lights he staggered to his feet.

'I . . . ' he gagged. 'I . . . '

'Felix! Are you all right?' That was Avril. He tried to answer and then, suddenly, vomited the contents of his stomach.

2

The woman smelt of the ineffable perfume of hospitals, a blend of soap and starch, iodoform and anaesthetics and yet, mingled with the clean, utilitarian scent, was the subtle, basic odour which turns a woman from a female machine into a thing of romance and excitement, a blend of flowers and night, the perfume of femininity.

Felix opened his eyes.

The tips of her fingers were cool to his skin as she touched his wrist and, with a strange detachment, he studied the curve of her cheek, the high, aristocratic nose, the full, sensuous mouth. Like Avril she wore her hair close-cut to her head and the style gave her a severe beauty.

She noticed his opened eyes.

'Hello, there! Feeling better?'

'What happened?' Felix swallowed and tried to sit upright. He was, he discovered, naked but for a pair of abbreviated shorts and lay on a bed made of smooth canvas stretched taut over a metal frame. A hard pillow rested beneath his head and a single blanket covered his body.

'You went under. I'm Doctor Brittain, by the way. Everyone calls me Gloria.'

'Did I pass out?'

'Not exactly.' She released his wrist. 'When I was a young girl,' she said, 'I loved fairs. I liked to ride the round-abouts and all those devices which throw you this way and that, upside-down and over, you know the kind of thing. I loved them — but I couldn't ride them for long. I used to get terribly ill.'

'Me too,' he said, then understood. 'Is that what happened to me?'

'Something like that. All your life you have been used to a constant of gravity. Your reflexes are adjusted to a regular pull and your sense of balance is a delicate mechanism on which you rely. Up here everything is different. Your eyes tell you that a thing is a yard away but to your muscles it is only six-inches. The co-ordination of the body finds itself at variance with the mental impulse-signals and sensory impressions. The result is an inner conflict as they try to adjust themselves.

'I understand.' He stared at the shadowed wall. 'Does everyone suffer this way?'

'More or less. The trick is to take things quietly for a while.'

'Which I didn't.' He frowned then put into words something which bothered him. 'You may think me very rude or very stupid but what you've just said doesn't make sense. Men have experienced zero-gravity without suffering ill effects.'

'That is quite true.' To his relief she didn't seem annoyed. 'But in zero-g there is not the same conflict. Those experiencing it do not try to walk, act and move as they would on Earth. And there is something else. When you were small didn't you ever envy those of your friends who could spend hours on the swings and roundabouts without ever feeling ill?'

He nodded.

'It effects some more than others. I suppose you rode up under sedation?'

'Yes. The usual thing. Scopolamine to ease the tension and pentathol to knock you out. By the time I recovered we were well on our way. From then on it was just a matter of waiting in the cocoon until we landed.' He gave an apologetic smile. 'I'm sorry.'

'For what? Asking questions?' She shook her head. 'As a scientist you should know better. The universe is one big question mark and the only way we can get the answer is to ask questions. No scientist should ever be reluctant to ask what he wants to know.'

'I agree, but I'm no scientist.'

'No?'

'I'm a mechanic.' He told her what he had told the others, then felt a sudden panic. 'Did you give me anything when I was ill?' He forced himself to sound casual, as if it were of minor interest. 'You did tell me to ask if there was anything I wanted to know,' he reminded.

'Asking doesn't always mean that you'll receive an answer,' she pointed out, then shrugged. 'Not that it matters. I gave you a sedative and you slept for several hours. While you were asleep I gave you something to reduce your pulse-rate; your heart will make automatic compensation if it has not already done so. If you should feel light-headed in the future, an almost semi-intoxicated feeling, then let me know.'

'I will,' he promised. 'Is there anything else I should be warned against?'

'Warned?' She looked at him, an odd expression in her blue eyes. 'That's an odd word to use.'

'Sorry,' he said quickly. 'That was rather loose terminology. I meant fore-warned, naturally.'

Inwardly he cursed himself for a fool. He, of all people, to make such a stupid mistake. With anyone else it wouldn't have mattered, it would have passed for a slip of the tongue. But to Doctor Gloria Brittain there was no such thing as a slip of the tongue. To a psychiatrist there never was.

He knew that all too well.

★   ★   ★

It had begun when he was twelve and had discovered how words could defeat a bully's strength. It was a time when the psychological aspects of advertising moulded itself into a science and the field offered rich rewards to a young man, so he had studied until sickened by the naked cynicism of the trade. Then had come the long files of mentally tormented men and women whom he had helped to a fuller life.

At thirty he had won fame by averting the engineers' strike — breaking the apparently impossible impasse with a neat, face-saving formula, and the government had begun to take an interest. That interest grew when, by luck, he had been at Dartmoor during the riot and had turned what could have been murderous fury into jeers, cat-calls and grumbling. Then had come the Portsmouth Mutiny and finally the interview with Sir Joshua Aarons.

But there was something wrong with the image of Sir Joshua. He was distorted, the heavy features wavering as if seen through water and his voice rolled echoingly along an endless tunnel.

' . . . *a delicate situation, Larsen, but*

we dare not take any chances . . . chances . . . chances . . . '

Felix wondered why the room was so hot.

' . . . something odd on the Moon. I don't want to tell you too much in case I influence your judgment . . . judgment . . . judgment . . . ' Then louder. *' . . . Seldon will help . . . help . . . '*

He was, of course, talking about Luna Station.

' . . . Security is concerned and we have to be certain . . . certain . . . certain . . . '

The image wavered even more and the rolling voice faded among the echoes.

' . . . go up there and look around . . . around . . . around.'

And then, very faintly.

' . . . traitors . . . traitors . . . traitors . . . traitors . . . '

Felix jerked upright, eyes wide in the darkness, feeling the hammering of his heart as he started awake. He had thrown off the blanket and was wet with perspiration and his throat was parched. Clumsily he fumbled for the light, the soft glow searing his eyes so that he squinted and shadowed his face with his hand.

He suspected that he had been poisoned.

Nursing his throbbing temples he reviewed the past few hours. The initial sickness was, he admitted, probably a normal consequence of too much exertion too soon after landing. But that sickness would have passed, certainly, despite the doctor's facile explanation, it should not have left him so weak and ill.

But, if he had been poisoned, it was too late to worry about it now.

Cautiously he swung his legs over the edge of the bed and lunged for the door. He needed water and there was no faucet in the room. Outside he blinked at the sun-glare of the lights and stood, swaying a little, wondering which way to go.

'Felix!' Avril stood before him, her face anxious. 'Is anything wrong?'

'What are you doing here?'

'I dropped by to see if you were all right.' Unconsciously her eyes fell from his face to his near-naked body. He was in excellent physical condition despite his age and didn't suffer from false modesty.

But, for some reason, her interest angered him.

'Water,' he said. 'I want some water.'

'Down here.' She led him down the passage to a bathroom. 'Washing facilities, a shower, all the usual essentials. Do you want me to help you?'

'No.'

He plunged into the room and discovered a faucet over a bowl. He rinsed his mouth and laved his face and neck and then gulped water. Finally, when he could hold the water without retching, he stripped off his shorts and stepped under the shower.

The water was ice-cold and he cringed from the impact but resisted the impulse to heighten the temperature. There were no towels but a vent blasted him with hot air when he stood before it on a switchmat. A dispenser over the wash bowl yielded a depilatory cream and he removed his stubble. Then, clean and dressed and feeling much more capable, he stepped into the corridor.

Avril was waiting for him.

'That's better!' She made no effort to

hide her admiration. 'You know, Felix, you're quite a man.'

He nodded, not answering.

'You're mad at me.' She slipped her arm through his. 'If you want to take a crack at me then go ahead but don't get all distant and frozen. I wouldn't like that.'

'Forget it.' He halted outside his door. 'Thank you anyway.'

'For showing you the toilet?' She looked at him from under her eye lashes. 'That was no trouble at all.'

'I didn't mean that.' He pushed open the door. 'I meant for coming to see if I was all right. It was good of you to bother.'

'I'm just selfish,' she said. 'I was protecting something I want very much.' She moved closer to him, her eyes very bright and her lips very soft. 'Would you like me to come inside?'

Her directness startled him, used as he was to blatant invitations and he fumbled for a face-saving excuse to refuse her offer.

'That would be nice,' he said, 'but

there's no lock on the door.'

'Of course there is, silly.' She showed him, a thin strip of metal slid from the panel into a catch. 'See? No one will bother us here, not that it matters if they do.' Her breathing, he now noticed had accelerated.

'Some other time.'

He stepped past her into the room, closing and locking the door, leaning against it as a sudden return of nausea welled within him.

Damn her, he thought. Damn her and her long, nice route march designed to make him sick so that he could be doped and questioned. If he had been questioned. The chances were that he had but he hoped his conditioning would have stood up to any techniques the doctor may have used.

He sighed and settled on the bed, adjusting the hard pillow and covering himself with the single blanket. The light stung his sensitive eyes and he snapped it out, staring into the warm darkness. The darkness was a friend and he frowned as he recognised the symbolism, the dark, all-embracing, all-protecting womb.

It was, he thought, no way for a very special agent of Her Majesty's Government to feel.

3

The woman at the office smiled and said: 'Hello, Felix, feeling better?'

'Yes, thanks.' News obviously travelled fast in the station. 'Is Sir Ian available?' He misunderstood her hesitation. 'Doctor Brittain . . . Gloria, passed me as fit and told me to report here.'

'I know. She called through and said that you were ready for work. It's just that Sir Ian is engaged with the Commission at the moment and I . . . '

She broke off as Macdonald, together with the members of the visiting team, emerged from an inner door. He recognised Felix at once.

'Larsen! It's good to see you on your feet again!'

'Not as glad as I am to be on them, Sir Ian.'

'I can imagine.' The Director smiled. 'Well, I suppose you're all ready and eager to get on with the job, eh?'

'The sooner the better,' said Felix then, delicately. 'Did you happen to read my papers, Sir Ian?'

'I glanced at them.' Macdonald looked thoughtful. 'You will be working with Major Crombie for the most part but he is engaged at the moment. Have you had a chance to look over the station?'

'Hardly, Sir Ian.'

'Of course you haven't. Silly of me to ask. Well, I'll tell you what, we are about to look over some of the laboratories, the bio-physical ones. If these gentlemen have no objection you could tail along at the rear.'

They had no objection and Felix followed the little procession as it wound through the corridors. He wondered how the status-conscious members of the Commission must feel at the Director's action. They had hardly been in a position to refuse without causing friction but Macdonald had made it very clear that he regarded Felix as being more important than they. For a man of Macdonald's political experience it was an odd thing to do.

An armed guard stood before a sealed door and he snapped to attention as Macdonald halted before him.

'Inform Professor Ottoway that the Royal Commission would like to inspect his laboratories,' said Macdonald. He turned to the others as the guard spoke into one of the ubiquitous intercom boxes.

'Certain areas of the station are restricted to casual visiting,' he explained. 'The atomic pile, the stores, these laboratories, the food rooms and, naturally, the biochemical laboratories, arsenal and hospital.'

'Why the hospital?' Meeson was curious but General Watts had the answer.

'Drugs,' he said curtly. 'Right, Sir Ian?'

'Correct, General. We have quite a large supply of various drugs and narcotics here and we have no intention of taking any chances.' He faced the door as it swung open and Ottoway stood facing them.

Felix's first impression of the man was one of anger. It was a deep, smouldering, clamped-down rage which revealed itself in a slight narrowing of the eyes and a betraying tension of the mouth. An untrained man would have missed it and would have merely thought that the scientist was consumed with impatience, but to Felix the signs were plain.

'Professor Ottoway, I think you have met these gentlemen before. They would like to see your laboratories.'

'Certainly.' Ottoway stepped to one side. 'Will you please enter, gentlemen.'

They shuffled through the narrow door and for a moment Felix stared directly into the bio-physicist's eyes.

'I'm just along for the ride,' he said easily. 'I hope you don't mind.'

'Should I?'

'Well, I don't suppose you welcome a lot of ignorant laymen stamping over your working space, Reg.' He held out his hand. 'By the way, I'm the new boy around here.'

'I know.' For a moment Ottoway hesitated, then his hand gripped Felix's. 'We must have a chat when this lot's over. Now I'd better get on with the guided tour.'

It was, like most tours of laboratories, a matter of looking blankly at unfamiliar apparatus and listening to those who knew trying to tell those who didn't just what was done in such places. Felix had expected no different but he was due for a surprise.

'This is the last room.' Ottoway opened a door. 'This is where we keep Abic.'

He ushered them inside to where a glistening apparatus bulked large in the centre of the chamber.

* * *

It was a box, thirty cubic feet of sterile plastic from which snaked a complex of wires, tubes and conduits. It stood on a metal frame rigidly bolted to the floor and the frame was sturdy enough to support a small military tank. A grid of metal bars protected the box and beneath, housed in the framework, humped machinery glistened with the sheen of crystal and polished alloy. The entire installation was a master-piece of technical engineering.

It must have cost, Connor knew, a fortune.

'What is it?' he asked.

'This is Abic.' Ottoway turned to the other occupant of the room. 'Professor Jeff Carter,' he introduced. 'Jeff, I think you know everyone here.'

'Pleased to meet you.' Jeff gave a mechanical smile which quickened into life as he saw Felix. 'So we meet again! Feeling better?'

'Yes, thank you.'

'Good.' Jeff smiled again, his eyes locking with those of the Director for a moment before he stepped back. Someone cleared his throat.

'Just what,' said Lord Severn blandly, 'is Abic?'

'Artificial Biochemical Integration Computor,' said Ottoway. 'We had to twist words a little to arrive at a pronounceable diminutive.'

'I see. What does it do?'

'Nothing.'

'I beg your pardon!'

'It doesn't do anything,' repeated Ottoway impatiently. 'It's just a great big

35

brain in a box. We have grown it from the basic elements of life and we feed it with synthetic blood but it doesn't do anything.'

'That,' said General Watts, 'doesn't seem to make very much sense.'

'Pure research rarely does seem to make sense, General, but without it we would still be in the Dark Ages.' Ottoway leaned against the guard rail. 'What you are seeing in this laboratory could be the founding of an entirely new branch of science. As a Military man, General, you can surely see the advantages to be gained if we can learn how to regenerate the human body.'

'I don't understand,' confessed Prentice. 'Just what do you mean by that?'

'Every living thing holds within itself the ability to heal its injuries but with the higher orders, men for example, that healing ability is 'wild'. By that I mean the new tissue is not the same as the old. A cut will heal but it will become a scar and scar tissue is not as efficient as ordinary cellular growth. Bones are never as good as they were, once broken. An ear, or limb, is lost forever if severed or damaged too badly and, of course, nerves never grow at all under any circumstances.'

'I follow you.'

'The lower orders, starfish, lobsters, simple organisms like that, heal much better than we do. They 'regenerate'. Cut a starfish into pieces and each piece will grow into a complete starfish. If a lobster loses a limb, a claw for example, it will grow a new claw. If we had the same ability we could grow new eyes, new limbs if we had to.' He glanced at the enigmatic box. 'Abic may help us learn how to do that.'

'How?' Meeson was blunt.

'We have grown a brain. It's only a question of time before we learn how to grow other organs.'

Meeson surprised them with his knowledge. 'Tissue has been grown before,' he said. 'But without the results you so confidently claim.'

'That is true,' admitted Ottoway. 'But when you say that tissue has been grown you mean that living tissue, from a chicken's heart, has been kept alive and has shown natural growth. Abic isn't like that. We have, quite literally, created living tissue from the basic nucleic acids DNA and RNA. That makes what is in this box quite unique. I call it a brain because it has minute cell-structure, contains an electric potential and registers various patterns on an encephalograph. Jeff, show them some of the records.'

Jeff Carter, his widow's peak and flared eyebrows accentuating the Mephistophelian appearance he assiduously cultivated, handed round strips of narrow graph-paper.

'They are not facsimiles of what would be recorded from a human brain,' pointed out Ottoway. 'There are five distinct wave-patterns and the alpha line, the one in red, shows a peculiarly erratic fluctuation.'

'Interesting.' General Watts handed back his roll of paper; he had hardly glanced at it. 'I can see this could be an interesting scientific experiment but isn't it rather a costly one?'

'Very costly,' said Connor. Ottoway flushed.

'I'm afraid I don't understand,' he snapped. 'Cost surely, is a relative term. What we hope to do here may well affect the future of every human creature on the face of the Earth — and beyond. I fail to see how anyone with an ounce of imagination can think of money in such a context.'

★   ★   ★

Ottoway had gone too far. Men, especially such men as these, were not accustomed to being made to look and feel cheap and small. Stepping forward from where he had watched quietly from the rear Macdonald did his best to smooth things over.

'Professor Ottoway has rather strong views on the subject, gentlemen.' His tone and smile gave them to understand that he too had had his share of dealing with the vagaries of long-haired scientists who seemed to hold common men in contempt.

'So I gather.' Watts wasn't to be easily mollified. Neither was Connor.

'I'm rather surprised, Sir Ian,' he said waspishly, 'that you've permitted such expenditure on what is apparently a scientific novelty totally divorced from the real function of the station.'

'Now, gentlemen.' Lord Severn, despite his own feelings in the matter was the born aristocrat. Quarrelling, if there were to be quarrels, should be in private and not before members of the staff.

'Reg has done it now,' whispered a voice in Felix's ear. Jeff stood close beside him. 'A damn shame, though, to put Sir Ian in a mess. If he's got any sense he'll apologise and do it fast.'

'Do you think he will?'

'I don't know. He doesn't like those stuffed-shirts, but who does? But he might do it to keep the peace.'

Privately Felix doubted it. The repressed rage he had sensed in the bio-physicist needed an outlet and it had found one. It would take a tremendous effort of will to control that rage and he didn't think Ottoway was capable of it. The man proved him wrong.

'I'm sorry,' said Ottoway. 'Lord Severn,

General Watts, Mr. Connor, please accept my apologies for an unpardonable outburst. Sir Ian, the rest of you, the same.'

When Ottoway did a thing, thought Felix, he didn't stop half-way. But the man hadn't finished.

'I feel I owe you all an explanation.' He gave an apparently rueful smile, but Felix recognised it for the sneer it really was. 'It's just that, when I think of the fantastic sums we are spending to ensure the total annihilation of humanity then no expenditure to save them can be considered too much. But this is a private view and, again, I beg your pardon.'

He had, if anything, made matters worse. Quickly Macdonald changed the subject.

'I should point out that Abic, though a monumental discovery, is really only a by-product of our main line of research. It is, however, one which promises to develop into a tool of extreme scientific and financial value. Professor Ottoway?'

For a moment Felix thought he would refuse then, taking a deep breath, he did as the Director had asked.

'Look on it as a computer,' he said abruptly. 'You know what they are, big, limited and expensive. Now the human brain is small and, as far as we know, we only use a part of it so that the effective mechanism can be held in the hollow of your hand. That mass of tissue is the finest computer known. It has an incredible memory-capacity. It has the ability to weigh probabilities and make decisions on the basis of both learned and assumed information. It controls a highly organised machine, the body, and it is self-maintaining; a human brain, even if aberrated, can still function. No machine built by man can do that.'

'But the soul?' Prentice was a regular church-goer and could not look on anything human as simply a machine.

'I am not interested in theological fantasies,' snapped Ottoway. 'I look on the brain as an instrument. Well — we have grown one just like it.'

'What the professor means,' said Macdonald, 'is that we have discovered a method of actually growing a computer-type device. I need hardly point out the obvious advantages of such a mechanism. The saving in manpower alone would be colossal not to mention the cost of components and I need scarcely remind you, General, what it would mean in a military sense.'

He was hitting below the belt, appealing to Watts' military nature and making him, if only reluctantly, an ally. It was a practical use of applied psychology and even Connor, the mean-minded counter of figures was impressed.

4

There was no natural time on the moon. There was a fourteen day 'night' and an equal period of day on the surface but in the station it was always the same and time, by the old system, was merely a useful appendage to living; not something which controlled the hours of sleep and activity.

It was, to Felix, an interesting routine. Meals were always the same size, altering in variety but with nothing to differentiate breakfast, lunch, dinner or supper. The personnel ate when they felt the need of food and slept when sleep became a necessity. Most of the time they worked and when they relaxed it was usually to exercise at manual labour or to do work of choice rather than of schedule.

It was, he thought, a little like the hive of a colony of ants but without the sharp diversity of types to be found in either. There were men and women, all mature, all, apparently, well-adjusted. There were scientists and skilled technicians of both sexes. There were soldiers; again of both sexes but, aside from the insignia on their coveralls, there was no way of telling military and non-military personnel apart. Social barriers simply did not exist.

And, to any psychologist, that was all wrong.

It was wrong because it wasn't normal. No matter where men gather there is always demarkation. Either by colour, creed, wealth or responsibility, accent or intelligence there are always social barriers. Many of them would not apply in the station. All were, in various degrees, intelligent. They spoke very much alike. They seemed to share a common lack of interest in religion and such people would not be prejudiced against the colour of a man's skin. That he could accept but, after all, the station was a military establishment and there should have been a far stronger barrier between the military personnel and the others.

He mentioned it to Avril.

'Why should there be any difference?'

She was honestly puzzled at his question. 'We're all alike, aren't we?'

He had to admit that basic truth.

'Well, then?' She hugged his arm. 'Now that you've finished prowling all over the station how about letting me take you up to the Eyrie?'

'The Eyrie can wait!' He smiled to take the sharpness from his tone. It had been impossible to avoid the woman without being obviously unpleasant and he hesitated to make an enemy.

'You've been here a long time,' he said. 'Five years, isn't it?'

'Almost six. Why?'

'Think back,' he urged. 'Was it like this when you first came here?'

She frowned and absently tasted the meal she was supervising. Around them the kitchen was in its usual bustle and he felt an interloper but she had grabbed him in one of the corridors and, as she put it, 'made him walk her to work.'

'More salt,' she decided, and he wondered if she had forgotten his question. She read his expression.

'I was just thinking. No. No, I don't

think it was. We had separate messes and a lot of stupid regulations which didn't work anyway. So things just . . . well, just became as they are now.'

'When did that happen?'

'I don't know. I told you, it just seemed to happen. Why?'

'No reason, I'm just naturally curious.'

'I'd hardly call you that,' she said suggestively, then bit her lip at his frown. 'I'm sorry. I annoy you, don't I?'

'No, not really, but — '

'But what? Do you find me repulsive? Is that it?'

'Of course not!'

'Then what's the matter? Is there anything wrong in a person feeling the way I feel about you? I'm not ashamed of it. I can't understand why you . . . '

' . . . why I don't take what is offered?' He was deliberately crude. 'I eat when I'm hungry, Avril, don't you?'

She was not offended. 'I'm hungry now, Felix. How long must I wait?'

He sighed, not answering, wondering how to tell her how oddly outrageous her conduct seemed to him, fresh as he was from a society in which normal women simply did not express themselves so frankly. But he was in a different society now and one in which, he had learned by observation, her conduct was not outrageous at all.

But morals had nothing to do with his reluctance to become emotionally involved. He had to find Seldon!

★　★　★

Major Crombie entered the dining-room as he was about to leave. The officer caught his arm.

'Felix! I've been wanting to have a word with you. Come and join me.'

'I've just eaten, Major.'

'Well, have a cup of tea then. It's about time we had a talk.'

Felix waited as the Major fetched his food and the tea from the serving hatch. He looked sharply at Felix as he sat down. 'Having a spot of bother with Avril?'

'No, Major. Why do you ask?'

'The poor woman's crying her eyes out

back there.' He spooned food into his mouth, chewed, swallowed and gave a grunt. 'Damn nice woman, that. You're a lucky man if you but knew it.'

Felix remained silent, toying with his cup.

'I haven't had a chance to talk with you earlier,' said Crombie, still busy with his spoon. 'What with the Commission and the General keeping me busy there hasn't been the time. Still, from what I hear you haven't been twiddling your thumbs. What do you think of the station?'

'It's nice, once you get used to it,' said Felix drily. Crombie chuckled.

'It hit you harder than others,' he said, and pushed aside his empty plate. 'Adjusted now?'

'Perfectly, Major. You want to talk about the lasers, I take it?'

'Yes. From what Sir Ian tells me you've come to install some new weapons. Whitehall, naturally, hasn't told me a thing about it. Just what does their installation entail?'

'I shall need a plentiful source of power. The atomic pile can provide that, of course, but the cables will have to be protected against accident and enemy action. We'd better have two separate sources of supply; but you'll know about these details. The lasers, there are two of them, must be situated at strategic points from the viewpoint of defence and field of fire.'

'Range?' Crombie was laconic.

'Theoretically the range is infinite.' Felix smiled at the Major's expression. 'Just my joke, Major,' he apologised. 'They are energy weapons and, as a searchlight beam can be said to carry to infinity, so with the beam from a laser. However, the effective range is about ten miles.'

'On a line-of-sight, naturally.' Crombie nodded, his face thoughtful. 'Can they be geared to automatic sighting and firing mechanisms?'

'Yes, their main function will be to guard the approach to the station from missile attack. We can arrange for cross-linked firing and sighting devices for concentrated or dispersed defence together with variable aperture — I'll go

50

into that once they're installed.'

'Good. Now about the positioning? I know the territory better than you do, of course, and . . . '

Crombie was wrong but Felix didn't tell him so. He'd studied the contour map of the area and experts had decided on the exact location of the weapons. He had learned those locations together with the reason for their choice when he had suffered the forced-tuition which had left him with an aching head but a complete knowledge of the theory and practice of the lasers. As long as he steered clear of technical discussions with electronic experts he would have no trouble in maintaining his cover.

Crombie's next words gave him a shock.

'You will be staying here to supervise their operation and maintenance, of course, and that brings up the question of your exact status.'

'How so, Major?'

'If you're military,' explained Crombie, 'you come under my orders but if you're a civilian technician then you come under

Sir Ian's. Not that it makes any real difference, you understand. In any case of emergency I take full command anyway, but it's as well to have these things straight.'

The Major, Felix realised, assumed that he was to be a permanent member of the community on the standard five-year minimum contract, and so must Sir Ian and all the rest of the station personnel.

'Surely my papers make my position clear,' said Felix quickly, and wondered if Sir Joshua had changed even more of what he had been given to understand. 'I come under Sir Ian as a civilian technician.'

Despite Crombie's assurance that it made no difference he knew better and he wanted to make his position clear from the start.

★   ★   ★

Crombie finished his tea and came to a decision.

'We'll go up to the Eyrie,' he said. 'You haven't been up there yet, have you?'

'No, Major. But you know that.'

'I do? How?'

Felix smiled and gently shook his head.

'I am a stranger on the station,' he said. 'You are the military commander. Are you honestly going to tell me that there isn't a move I've made that you haven't been kept informed about? If so then you are failing your duty and that I simply refuse to believe.'

It was a risk but a calculated one. Felix had no desire to appear stupid and it was obvious that, as he had pointed out, Crombie would have done his job. But he wasn't simply trying to flatter the Major.

He was conscious, as every spy is conscious, and he was, in a sense a spy, of the thin line of danger between knowing too little and knowing too much; of being too curious and not curious enough. It was better for him to gain a reputation for shrewd inquisitiveness than dull nosiness. The former held the lesser risk.

For Felix needed information and, unless he could contact Seldon, he could only get it by asking questions. Those questions had to be hidden so as to disguise his true intent.

For a moment Crombie stared at him from hard, blue eyes, then he smiled.

'You're a shrewd one!'

'I'd be a fool if I couldn't see the obvious,' said Felix. 'But, as you know, I haven't been up to the Eyrie.'

'Then it'll be an experience for you.' Crombie chuckled, accepting the change of subject. 'Though, if Avril has her way, you'll be going up there quite a lot in the future. It's a favourite place for romance, you know, Earthlight and all that.' He sighed with obvious reminiscence. 'Well, you'll see.'

They climbed to the Eyrie and, as Crombie had promised, Felix found it an experience. Even after a short time in the low gravity his body had become so adjusted that to exert his full strength needed a conscious effort. The yard-high stairs seemed monstrous at first but he soon adapted.

'Good exercise,' puffed Crombie when they were half-way up. 'It's important to keep in good condition.'

It was obvious why. One day they

would return to Earth and there, unless fit, would be crushed by the greater gravity. Muscles, if allowed to grow weak, would refuse the additional burden. There was more than one reason for climbing to the Eyrie.

'There it is.' Crombie gestured to the window as they entered the room. 'Not bad, eh?'

'Very good.' Felix had left home too short a while to be homesick but he was impressed. 'When was this room built, Major?'

'Not too long ago. Why?'

'Just curiosity. It must have been a tremendous effort to bore that shaft.'

'Yes. Yes, I suppose it was, but we all joined in. Off-duty exercise, you know, something to keep us from getting soft. We're always digging and working at something like this.' He pointed at the window.

'From here we've a clear view right to Tycho, that's that long mound on the horizon. Now, if we set the lasers at about this level, set them in the face to either side, for example, we'll be able to cover the ground with cross-fire as well as an almost vertical cone. You agree?'

'It's hard to say.' Felix squinted through the window, his face pressed against the crystal. 'The bulk of the mountain protects the rear but we don't want to limit the field of fire more than is essential. I'll have to go outside.'

'Of course.' Crombie was affable. 'I'll have Sergeant Echlan arrange a detail and we can discuss it again after you've had a chance to study the ground.' He hesitated. 'That is unless you'd rather have a technical detail?'

'No. Not at first, anyway. It's a military matter and I'd prefer military personnel.'

'Glad to hear it,' beamed the Major. 'Technical men are too concerned with engineering problems in terms of supply and construction rather than military necessity. Why, I remember one time when . . . '

His voice rambled on but Felix wasn't consciously listening. He stood by the window, looking down at the vista outside, but his thoughts were elsewhere. He was thinking of a certain type of psychotic personality, a symptom of which was a necessity and a delight in looking down from high places.

A paranoid personality with delusions of grandeur — one of the most explosively dangerous forms of insanity known.

5

The intercom hummed a series of notes and Crombie broke off his reminiscences.

'That's for me,' he said, and crossing to the instrument, pressed the button with a spatulate thumb. 'Yes?'

'General Watts would like to see you, Major. He is waiting in control.'

'Thank you. I'll be right down.' He shrugged as he met Felix's eyes. 'Back to the grind,' he said disrespectfully. 'Well, maybe I can manage to persuade the General to send me up some real weapons instead of the toys I'm supposed to defend this place with. It's worth another try.'

'That shouldn't be a problem.' Felix fell into step with the Major as he moved towards the door. 'Couldn't you get some from the Americans?'

'That's what the General keeps telling me,' grumbled Crombie, 'but I don't like begging and there's a snag. The Yanks are willing to defend us, no doubt about that, but they want to do it their way. They want to send us weapons and men both.'

'That seems reasonable. Their base is too far away for them to get here in a hurry with ground forces. What's the objection?'

'To operate efficiently they'll have to have a permanent garrison here at the station and we don't want that.' Crombie's face tightened and, studying him, Felix saw something of his true nature. 'Britain shouldn't have to rely on anyone. This station is ours, built with our own hands and we want to keep it independent. We can't do that if we're saddled with a foreign garrison no matter how close they are as allies.'

'I see your point. Does the General agree?'

'The General,' said Crombie grimly, 'is too concerned with avoiding treading on certain political toes. Damn it, no soldier should ever get mixed up with politics, it's a dirty game at the best of times.'

'But a pact — ?'

'A pact merely means that you've got to

do what the other fellow wants you to do when he wants you to do it.' Crombie gave a disgusted snort. 'And what kind of a pact is it when you've no option? Any soldier worth his salt knows that you can't buy friends. You have to earn them and you can only do that if you have independence. No one respects a lap-dog.'

Felix knew better than to argue. The Major had revealed an unsuspected stubbornness and he began to understand why he had been chosen to command the military garrison on the moon. Britain's true strength depended on just such men as the Major.

'You'd better go and inspect the suits,' Crombie said as they reached the top of the slide. 'Ross is in charge of them, a good man at the job. Tell him I sent you and that he's to look after you.' He hesitated at the opening of the spiral tube. 'Do you want to go first?'

'After you, Major.'

'Can't say that I blame you.' Crombie settled himself into position and grinned up at Felix. 'Every time I ride down this thing I wonder if I'm going to arrive safe at the other end. Well, here goes! See you at the bottom!'

He released his hold and vanished with a soft slither of clothing against the polished stone. Felix waited a moment then settled himself on the slide, holding on for a few seconds to give the other man a chance to get well ahead. Then he let go.

It was a startling experience. Centrifugal force flung him hard against the winding wall of the slide as he plunged endlessly down through the solid darkness. Then, just as he wondered if the ride would ever end, the slide evened out and he slowed to a halt as lights stabbed at his eyes. Blinking he rolled to his feet and met the Major's grin.

'Like it?'

'It's something I'd imagine you have to get used to.'

Felix was a little shaken by the descent. 'Is there another way down?'

'Only by the stairs but no one ever uses them.' Crombie pointed down one of the radiating corridors. 'You'll find Ross down that way close to the hangar. O.K.?'

'I'll find it,' promised Felix, and dusted himself down as the Major moved away.

He was too optimistic. Even though he had wandered over the station he had yet to learn the maze-like windings by heart and he tended to get confused by the sameness of the corridors. With a shock he realised that he had reached the foot of the stairs leading up to the Eyrie. They were necessarily some distance from the foot of the slide and he must have taken the wrong turning. He frowned, wondering just how to retrace his steps and then, with a shrug, began to climb the stairs.

He was in no hurry to inspect his suit, the exercise would do him good and he wanted to experience the thrill of descent again. None of those reasons accounted for the speed with which he raced up the stairs. He was panting when he reached the top but did not hesitate to jerk open the door of the room. It swung hard behind him, slamming against his rear and thrusting him forward. He didn't notice the blow.

A woman was standing before the

window and she was being strangled to death.

★ ★ ★

She stood very still, very calm, almost as if unaware of the hands which so savagely gripped her throat. Only her eyes, lustrous in her almond-shaped face, moved sidewise towards the soft thud of the closing door. For a moment the tableau held then her companion, a thin, haggard-looking soldier, realised they were not alone.

His hands fell from the woman's throat, the left arm hiding the name lettered on his coverall. He stared at the woman, then at Felix, then back to the woman. He made a peculiar, sobbing, animal-like sound deep in his throat and rushed blindly across the room.

'Wait!'

Felix made a grab at the man and was thrust aside with frenzied strength. He staggered, flung himself at the door and ran outside just in time to see the man vanish down the slide. Grimly he returned to the woman. Her name, he saw, was Shena Dawn.

'Are you all right?'

'Yes, thank you.' Her voice was soft and held the trace of a lilting brogue. She was very beautiful in a black-haired, earthy kind of fashion.

'Who was that man?'

'A friend.'

'Some friend. He tried to kill you.'

'You think so?' She swallowed, frowned and touched the slender column of her throat. Angry against the smoothness of her skin, the marks of fingers told of the relentless pressure that had been used. Eyes narrowed she explored her injuries; more upset at the threat to her beauty than at her narrow escape.

'The marks will fade.' Felix examined the angry welts. 'The pressure was constant. There might be a little bruising and some soreness but nothing serious.'

'Good.' Her composure was incredible. 'Then there's no harm done.'

'No harm!' Felix was baffled. 'Look,' he said as if speaking to a child. 'You don't seem to realise what has happened. That man intended to kill you.' She could, he thought, be suffering from shock. It would explain her indifference.

'But he didn't.'

'Only because of the sheerest luck,' he snapped. 'If I hadn't arrived when I did you would be dead by now. Can't you understand that?'

'Of course I can.' She smiled, showing perfect teeth and expanded her chest in a deliberate gesture that was almost as old as the human race. 'But I can't see what you are so serious about. You did arrive and he didn't kill me. That's all there is to it.'

'Not quite. He could try again.'

Her smile irritated him. He was close enough so that he could see there was no dilation of the eyes and, when he touched her wrist, her pulse was normal. She was not suffering from shock.

The woman, he realised, was actually enjoying the experience and he thought he knew why. She had never consciously accepted the threat of personal extinction so that, to her, she had never been in any real danger at all. The man had been demonstrating emotion, that was all and she probably found it amusing rather than anything else. He knew better.

The man had intended murder. Both instinct and training told Felix that there could be no mistake about that. He had seen his face, illuminated from the light from the window, and it had been a killer's mask.

'This man,' he said casually. 'Is he a serious type?'

'Who, Colin?' She looked thoughtful. 'I suppose you could call him that. He certainly can't take a joke.'

'It wouldn't have been a joke if I hadn't arrived on the scene.'

'But you did.'

'Only by chance. I still don't know what really brought me up here.'

'So?'

'So, damn it, you were almost murdered!' Her calmness was exasperating. Even if she were inwardly convinced that she had not been in danger her reactions were all wrong. She laughed and that made it worse.

'If pigs had wings they would fly,' she

said. 'If you're going to worry about all the things that might have happened but didn't then you'll have no time to live at all.' Her hand, resting on his arm, tightened with a gentle hint of intimacy. 'If you've got to have a reason then I can give you one. You were impelled to climb up here in order to save a maiden from distress.'

'All right.' He accepted defeat. 'What was the quarrel about anyway?'

'Nothing important.' Her smile was purely feline, 'The poor man thinks he owns me, I can't see why. Silly, isn't it?'

It was more than silly. Only a blind, infatuated fool would ever hope to think that she could ever be faithful to one man. Felix knew the type too well.

He had met them before; women who took a sadistic delight in their power over men and who used sex as a weapon of conquest rather than as a thing of personal satisfaction. They played the field and continued to do so until age or the accident of finding someone too intense terminated their career. Age rendered them harmless but too often they met an unnatural death and some poor devil paid for his infatuation by suicide or the scaffold.

As Colin would have done had Felix not arrived in time.

He grew thoughtful at the sudden shift of perspective. Until this moment he had regarded his almost accidental reclimbing to the Eyrie as benefiting only the woman but she wasn't the only one concerned. Had he not lost his way downstairs and yielded to an inexplicable impulse, the woman would have died — but so also would the man, either by suicide through remorse or by the due process of law.

Suddenly he felt an imperative, almost overpowering need of haste.

'His name,' he said sharply. 'What is his name?'

'You're a funny one. It's Maynard but — '

'Thanks.' He gave her the kiss she obviously expected, a swift pressure of his lips and then released her.

'Felix! When am I . . . '

He didn't hear the rest. The door thudded behind him as he jumped on the slide and, as he whirled into darkness, he scrubbed his mouth with the back of his hand.

★　★　★

A guard stood at the opening to the barracks. He was armed and looked bored as he leaned against the stone wall. Felix guessed that normally he wouldn't have been there at all but was window-dressing for the General. A bit of military bull which served no real purpose. He straightened as Felix approached.

'Halt!'

'I've halted.' Felix glanced past the guard to where corridors ran from a wide area. 'I'm looking for Colin Maynard. Where can I find him?'

'I don't know.' The guard lowered his rifle. 'I've only this minute come on duty,' he explained. 'Why don't you have him paged if you want to see him?'

'With the General around?'

'No. No, I suppose not.' The guard looked disgusted. 'Him and his mania for playing tin soldiers!'

69

'He probably passed the other guard,' said Felix. 'Where would his room be?'

'Down there, second on the right.' The guard hefted his rifle. 'But that's out of bounds now to all civilian personnel. The Major . . . '

' . . . won't know anything about it. I promise you.'

'But — hell, where's the sense? Go ahead then and make it snappy.'

Felix nodded, pushed past the guard and headed for the corridor inwardly thanking the logical mind of the guard who saw no good reason for dividing the station personnel into two species of humanity. The close affinity between military and non-military was not to be easily broken if it could ever now be broken at all.

He reached the corridor and stared at the line of matching doors, each with its single name. Running along the passage Felix glanced at the neat lettering.

He couldn't be absolutely certain that Maynard would be in his room but it was a logical assumption. A wounded creature will always return to its lair and the man had been deeply wounded in the psyche if not in the flesh. His room would be the only place where he could be certain of privacy and which he could really call his own.

'Maynard!'

The door was locked but that was to be expected. It opened inward which made things that much easier but Felix didn't make the mistake of throwing himself against it. That would have bruised his shoulder and made a lot of noise and, while he didn't care about his shoulder, he didn't want an audience. There was a more efficient way of tackling the problem.

Lifting his foot he rested it on the panel where he imagined the latch would be then, thrust with all the power of calf and thigh. The fragile catch tore from its socket and the door swung open.

Maynard didn't look up. He sat hunched on the edge of his bed, his eyes tormented in the pallor of his face which was contorted about the muzzle of the rifle he had thrust into his mouth. His left hand gripped the stock of the weapon and his right thumb rested on the curved trigger. He had, Felix guessed, been sitting in that position for some time.

'Maynard! Don't!'

He was too late. Even as Felix ran forward he saw the thumb depress the trigger and tensed himself for the expected crack of the explosion, the blood and brains which must come spurting from the shattered skull.

Nothing happened.

No shot, no blood, no broken body writhing in death throes on the bed. Nothing but the dry click of the firing pin.

'I . . . ' The rifle fell from the contorted mouth as Maynard lost control. He seemed numb, dazed with the mental acceptance of imminent destruction, still not fully aware that he was still alive. 'I . . . It didn't . . . '

Gently Felix took the rifle from his hands. He worked the bolt and stared at the tiny cartridge gleaming in the hollow of his hand.

On the primer, deeply gouged in the soft copper, the mark of the firing pin made a spot of shadow against the soft sheen of the metal.

6

General Klovis, commander of United States Star Base One, thoughtfully stripped the cellophane from a cigar and put it in his mouth. As commander he had certain privileges, one of them being the right to smoke at any time he chose, but it was a right he refused to use. A commander, he insisted, should have an affinity with his men and so he confined his cigar smoking to the few periods during the day when general smoking was permitted. He didn't know that far from being appreciated his self-imposed hardship was derided by his men. They took the logical line that if top brass couldn't do as they wanted then what was the use of being top brass? Also they didn't believe the General played fair even though the air-crews solemnly swore that it was so.

'It's been a long time,' said Klovis sombrely. 'Maybe that Limey ship is in trouble?'

'If they are they haven't asked for help.' Major Tune, the second in command, dragged hungrily at his cigarette. 'How about sending them a message?'

'No.'

'Why not? Pete's in position and it will only take a minute.'

Pete was the automatic radio-relay satellite orbiting the moon for, without the reflecting blanket of a heavy-side layer, radio communication was on line-of-sight only. It was just another problem men had to face when living in a vacuum.

Klovis shook his head. 'You're not thinking straight, Tune. If we radio an offer of assistance and they refuse then that ends it. If, on the other hand, we were to pay a personal visit we might learn something.' He rose and brushed cigar ash from his tunic. 'This needs careful handling, Major. Crombie is prickly when it comes to a question of territorial rights.'

Tune didn't smile but he felt like doing so. Like most of his compatriots he had little admiration for the British, privately thinking of them as the decadent remains of a once-great power. They had had their day and now there were other, new powers in the world. Russia, China, the African Confederacy, still weak as yet but promising to flower in the near future, the South American Republic and, of course, the United States.

And, for almost half a decade, the United States had considered itself to be the one great champion and protector of Western freedom. Against such power and against such an ideal the British contribution seemed small indeed. Tune did not stop to remember that, without the British, there would have been no freedom to defend. But politicians are notorious for short memories.

'Washington will want to know about that unscheduled landing,' he reminded as they left the office. 'They probably know already but if we can tell them about it we'll show we're on the ball.'

'Washington, Moscow, Peking, they'll want to know.' Klovis scowled. 'It's getting so that a man can't spit on this goddam moon without every nation wanting to know just why.'

His anger was artificial, a defence against his reluctance to act the spy. Naturally generous, like all his race, he did what had to be done but he didn't have to like it. And, unlike Tune, he actively admired the struggles of the British to retain their independence while, at the same time, confounded by their logic which refused to admit they didn't stand a snowball's chance in hell of going it alone.

'Break out the big runner,' he ordered. 'Load it with cigars — no, they don't smoke over there. Well, stack it with candy and junk for the chicks, magazines and such. There's no sense in going empty-handed.'

'How about the crew, General?' Tune looked hopeful and Klovis knew why, but there was no chance of both of them going and, for once, he intended to pull his rank.

'Just me and the driver and a relief,' he said. 'It'll be enough. No, wait! We'd better take Rasch while we're at it. He can be the relief driver. O.K.?'

'Right, General.' Tune moved away to supervise the readying of the ground-runner and Klovis could tell he was disappointed. It was odd how important the sight of a real woman became when they were not available.

* * *

It was a problem unique to the Americans. There were no women on their base. There were substitutes, busty, leggy pin-ups of females who were more anatomical freaks than normal women, but that was all. Klovis deplored the system but was powerless to do anything about it. The very prospect of tender young American girlhood being subjected to the brutal intimacy of soldiers was enough to bring every member of every woman's club screaming to her feet in angry protest. Even the logical alternative was equally condemned. The sanctity of marriage and the chastity of men were, to the vote-powerful women, of greater importance than their mental and physical well-being. And the politicians had no choice but to obey those who commanded the vote.

The results, even with a one-year change over, were predictable. Klovis knew that his problems of morale would be solved if he were permitted to mix his personnel. As it was he managed with a mixture of blindness, ignorance and hope.

Rasch was in his laboratory. He looked up as the General entered having walked more than a mile through a tunnel bored through the solid rock to a point where interference from the base apparatus would be at a minimum.

'Did you want me, General?'

'Later. How's it going?'

'As well as we can expect.'

Rasch leaned back in his chair. He was a thin, scholarly-looking man who wore rimless spectacles and who always seemed out of place in uniform. He was a ballistics expert but now he was in full charge of the paraphysical laboratory with the blessing of Congress who seemed to think it money well spent. Most of his waking hours were spent, with two assistants, in searching the unknown for the barely suspected. Klovis doubted if he would ever make any kind of an important discovery but his activities kept three men fully occupied and anything which kept men's minds from their own problems was, to the General, a thing to be encouraged.

'We've been getting more signals,' said Rasch after a moment. 'You remember I told you about them?'

Klovis nodded.

'They're odd things,' continued Rasch. 'They don't register on any of the apparatus we have to record the normal electromagnetic spectrum. They are erratic and vary in strength. It was only by sheer chance that we detected them in the first place.'

'Could they be messages?'

'They are on a telepathic level,' said Rasch. He, to Klovis's constant irritation, had a habit of simply ignoring anything said while he was in the middle of one of his discourses. 'At least,' he corrected himself, 'they are on a level which I have reason to suspect is that of emitted thought. Certainly they do not register on any other apparatus and the instruments I have devised do not respond to any regular radiation used in communication.'

'Can you actually register thought?' Klovis was doubtful. 'I mean, if you could you would actually be registering the presence of sentient life.'

'I am aware of that,' said Rasch primly. 'And, yes, I can register what can only be thought.'

'Telepathy?'

'No, not yet.'

'Then — ?'

'I can register a disturbance in the peculiar region I have named Zero X. The name means nothing and is only a label. Now, if this room were empty there would be zero stimulus and zero recording. When a person comes within range of the instrument it shows a decided reaction. That reaction comes directly from the mind.'

'Now wait a minute!' Klovis was no scientist but he wouldn't have been what he was if he were totally ignorant of other fields and he wouldn't have been where he was if he had known nothing of logic.

'That gadget of yours could be responding to the radiated heat of the body, the sonic beat of the heart or respiration, anything.'

'Please.' Rasch was offended. 'I have thought of, and eliminated, all those possibilities and many more you haven't even thought about. When I say that it reacts to mental thought that is exactly what I mean. But it doesn't mean that we have found a means of reading distant thoughts, though that may be the logical outcome of the discovery.'

'Heaven help us,' breathed Klovis. 'Why not?'

'There is too much noise. It is like listening to the traffic sounds of a city when you don't know what you are listening to. You hear a constant roar, not individual sounds, even though the roar is made up of an accumulation of parts.'

'All right.' Klovis was getting annoyed with the other's habit of impersonalised lecturing when asked a simple question. 'These signals you've been receiving, couldn't they have come from the base?'

'Impossible.'

'Are you going to tell me why?'

'The strength of the reaction. Even at full amplification I can only just register a mind within a short distance. These odd signals are tremendously strong — that is how I've managed to get a bearing on them.'

'You've what!'

'Taken a bearing.' Rasch was startled at the General's reaction. 'Didn't I tell you? I managed to rig up a few detectors and I've had them planted at various spots well outside the base. From then on it was only a matter of time before I obtained all the cross-bearings I needed to locate the source of the signals.'

'That proves it.' Klovis was bitter. 'The Reds have found a new method of sending signals. Won't Washington be pleased to hear this!'

'The Reds?' Rasch looked blank. 'What are you talking about, General? Where do they come in?'

'The signals! You tracked them back to their base, didn't you?'

'No. I didn't say that. They don't come from the Russians or the Chinese either.

Those signals come from our friends. They have their source in the British Station.'

* * *

The ground-runner wasn't the most comfortable means of transport ever devised but it wasn't too bad even over rough terrain. Giant wheels rose high above the rounded body their broad, edged treads clawing their way up inclines and supporting the weight of the machine over suspected patches of dust. That dust, powder-fine, could fill and hide quite deep craters and such traps were best avoided.

Inside it was clean, warm and relatively quiet, only the soft whine of the electric motors fed from ranked banks of powerful jangner batteries broke the silence as they drove the huge wheels. Leaning back in his cushioned seat General Klovis treated himself to a cigar.

'That's a nice smell, General.' The driver grunted as he dodged a shattered slide of detritus. 'Would it be all right if I had a smoke too?'

It wouldn't be all right and Klovis knew it. The air within the small cabin could only take a certain amount of contamination and if the driver had his way the smoking time would be cut by half.

'One cigarette,' he compromised. 'After that you chew gum and like it.'

'I'll chew it but I won't like it.' The driver lit his cigarette. 'How long are we staying, General?'

He was excited and Klovis knew why but he had bad news for the man.

'Not long. You're going to stay with the runner and get it recharged. Now I mean that! If I find you've been chasing those chicks I'll throw you in the brig!'

'Hell, General, can't a man have any fun?'

'Not that sort.' Klovis turned as Rasch came crawling from the rear. The man had taken the first drive-shift over the familiar ground around the base. Now, freshly awake, he looked like a myopic owl.

'God, the air's thick in here,' he

complained. 'I woke up thinking I was in a night club.'

'Have you ever been in a night club, Captain?' The driver, cigarette hanging from the corner of his mouth, scowled as he guided the vehicle. Deliberately he blew a plume of smoke against the viewport. Klovis crushed out his cigar.

'Smoking time's over,' he rapped. 'You heard me, driver.'

For a moment he was afraid the man would refuse and wondered just what he would do if he did. Any punishment would have to come later but what would he do if faced by outright mutiny? Shoot the man, he supposed. Both were armed but he doubted if he could bring himself to fire first. Then the man crushed out his cigarette and the danger was over. Yet, almost constantly, Klovis was aware of the too-thin barrier between obedience and defiance. Loyalty should have made that barrier stronger than steel but, on the moon, loyalty had a strangely empty sound.

'That's better,' said Rasch as the fans sucked the foul air through the conditioners. 'How much further have we to go?'

'A few hours yet. How about fixing some coffee and chow?'

The food, sealed in thermal containers, only needed the thrust of a thumb to break the seal and start the chemical reaction. They waited until the lids popped and the aroma of coffee and stew filled the compartment.

'Not bad.' Rasch spooned up the last of his food and drained his container of coffee. 'Do you think we'll be welcome, General?'

'I doubt it, but they can hardly refuse to charge our batteries and Macdonald isn't a bad type really.' Klovis looked at the driver. 'Do you want to stop and eat?'

'I can manage.' The driver ate with his eyes on the viewport, nursing his controls and temper both. Something, decided the General, would have to be done about him when they returned.

In the meantime he had other things to think about. If he hoped to learn anything about that mysterious ship he had to get inside the station and that meant having a reasonable excuse. The Director, he knew, was usually only too pleased to see him but that was when things were normal. No man can be expected to welcome an unwanted visitor especially if he is trying to hide something.

Klovis smiled as he thought over what Rasch had told him before they had left the base; pleased at the thought of the British having pulled a fast one in the field of communications. Then he sobered at an ugly thought. Liaison between their two countries was far too close for any such discovery to have remained a secret and, had it been developed in an allied laboratory to the point where it could be used then his base would be equipped with it now.

The alternative was that it had been developed by the common enemy and, if so, there was only one reason why those special signals had been tracked to the British station. An enemy agent was sending out secret information. Klovis had found his excuse.

7

High on the mountain above the station, five figures moved like tiny gleaming dolls in the full glare of the sun. They were roped in line and Felix, sweating with effort, was in the centre. Before him, inches from the viewport of his helmet, the eroded stone passed slowly downwards as he clawed his way up the steep slope.

A voice spoke quietly in his ear.

'Do you want to go to the same place as last time, Felix, or shall we try further to the right?'

That was Sergeant Echlan in charge of the detail which had accompanied Felix on each of his several 'inspection' trips to determine the positioning of the new weapons. One site had been chosen and he decided to settle on the other without further delay.

'The same place,' he said into the radio. 'It's about the best we can find within the working limitations.'

'Good.'

High above, the slope yielded to a crest of shattered stone before soaring again in crevassed escarpments. The crest hit a tiny plateau scored with crevasses and offered the best site available for the laser.

'It's going to be a hell of a job lugging the gear up here,' grumbled a voice. 'Let's hope they've packed it for portage.'

'We can drag it up with ropes if they haven't,' said another. 'Anyway, that isn't our grief. That's what technicians are for.'

Echlan cut across the chatter.

'Save your breath for climbing,' he snapped. 'Murray, wake up down there! Your rope is too slack!'

'Sorry, Sarge.'

'Let's get a move on. We're in direct sunlight, remember.'

It was one of the things Ross back at the Station had warned him about.

'Your body is generating heat all the time,' he'd told Felix. 'That heat can only be lost by radiation or conduction through the suit touching the rock. The suit is pretty well insulated so you're more likely to fry than freeze. But if you stay in direct sunlight too long you'll cook like an egg in boiling water, so stay in the shadow as much as possible.'

'I'll remember,' said Felix. 'Anything else?'

'Not much.' Ross had fussed with the suit as he adjusted it to size. 'The air supply is automatic and you'll be in constant radio communication with the station and with the rest of the party. The main thing is to keep calm no matter what happens. Panic can kill you. If anything goes wrong just sit tight and yell for help.' He'd stepped back, finally satisfied. 'Right, that should do it. Just keep it on and walk about for a while and you'll soon get used to it.'

It had taken less time than Felix had imagined to grow accustomed to the suit. Now, he felt quite an old hand.

Echlan reached the crest and drew himself over the edge snagging the rope around a jutting spur of rock. As Felix reached it in turn he admired the deft way the rope had been secured and guessed the sergeant was no stranger to mountaineering.

'You've climbed before,' he said and Echlan chuckled.

'We all have, Felix. Snowdon, Scarfell, even a spell attached to the Alpine Brigade.' His voice sharpened. 'Watch it there, Murray! Damn it man, watch where you're treading!'

The last man to reach the crest swayed then lunged forward as rock crumpled and fell from beneath his boot. The fragment fell, slowly to Felix's eyes, bounding down the slope and to the ground below.

'Clever!' Echlan was sarcastic. 'Are you trying to wear these mountains down on your very own, Murray? You could have given someone downstairs a nice head-ache.'

'I'm sorry, Sarge.'

'You should be. Well, let's get out of this sun.'

They dispersed, vanishing into patches of inky blackness adopting, Felix knew, the same defensive positions they did on each trip. It had taken him a while to

91

grow used to the system and he still found it a little amusing.

Echlan sat beside him, and he mentioned it.

'If you were a soldier you'd understand a lot better, Felix. Each time we come out we're on active service and have to act that way. If we ever do get attacked there'll be no time for extra training. That's why I went off at Murray. A thing like that could betray our position.'

'Do you think we'll ever be attacked?'

'I hope not, but there's always the possibility.' He hesitated. 'Maynard is back on duty now. Gloria reported him fit just before we left.'

'Good, I'm glad to hear it.' It was his turn to hesitate. 'He had a touch of migraine didn't he?'

Echlan chuckled softly as if to himself. 'Something like that,' he said, then: 'You're all right, Felix. You're all right.'

It was a compliment and he took it as such, knowing that it was the sergeant's way of thanking him for having used his discretion. Idly he wondered if Echlan guessed the truth and then knew that it was a stupid question. The sergeant knew his men and was far from being a fool. Gloria too had been discreet.

She had come at his call, assessed the situation in a glance and taken the numb and dazed soldier to the hospital. There, Felix guessed, she would have used drugs and hypnotherapy to ease the tormented mind and break the closed spiral of his emotional crisis. She had said nothing of the matter to Felix and he had said nothing to anyone else. The man was sick, that was all, and now he was better. The incident was closed.

The organism that was the station had healed itself.

★ ★ ★

'Let's get on with it.' Felix heaved himself to his feet and strode to the selected position. Carefully he plotted the site, marking the rock with wide streaks of chalk, finding it difficult to bend against the constriction of the suit.

'From here,' he pointed out, 'we can get a clear field of fire from a point just before the station to the extent of the range. We'll have to build defences for the laser and power supply is going to be something of a problem. We may have to drill a narrow shaft directly to the pile as well as run a buried cable.'

'How close to the station can we get?' Echlan moved towards the edge of the slope. Felix joined him.

'At a guess I'd say about where the rocket is standing now.'

'So far? Can't you get it closer than that?'

'Not unless we get too near the edge for safety. An explosive missile, for example, could crumble this entire area and undercut the position so that the whole thing will fall to the ground.'

'I see.' Echlan was thoughtful. 'So it's really a choice between using them for immediate defence or concentrating on missile attack.'

'That's about it,' agreed Felix. 'In a way that's the main trouble with a laser. A mortar could lob shells from strong cover and still remain unexposed but the effective destruction area of its shell is relatively small. The same with anti-missile guns, the delay-space between shells allows the oncoming missile to actually pass between them. The laser is effective from the projector to the target all along the beam. A synchronised cone of them make an almost impenetrable barrier.'

'I understand.' Echlan sounded thoughtful. 'Will you be all right here for a while? I want to check the area.'

'Go ahead, I won't be long.'

Alone Felix concentrated on what he was supposed to be doing. The area, even though previously selected, still needed on-the-spot surveying because, for example, no one had been able to tell beforehand that the area would be so friable. He frowned as he kicked at the crumbling rock. The site would have to be excavated down to solid stone and levelled. The defences would have to be built and camouflaged and there was always the problem of power-supply and maintenance.

He suddenly found that he was gasping and a little dizzy and realised that he had been standing too long in direct sunlight. Hastily he moved into a patch of shadow sprawling as if solid before a rock. The suit had a crude temperature-lowering device based on the chilling effect of expanding air but its use tended to deplete the air-supply and was more of an emergency measure than anything else.

The control was situated on his chest and he twisted it, feeling relief as a wave of coldness forced its way past his chest and over his face and head. Relaxing he leaned back and let his eyes drift over the edge towards the humped line of distant Tycho. They must be, he realised, almost at the level of the Eyrie. Far below the rocket ship looked like an expensive toy. Aside from the vessel the terrain looked as it must have always looked for uncounted thousands of years.

Something flashed in the distance.

Felix straightened, eyes narrowed behind the viewport as he searched the area. It had only been a brief twinkle of brilliance and for a moment he doubted whether he had seen anything at all. Then it came again, a sun-bright sparkle as of light reflecting from some bright surface. It came from the far distance between Tycho and the station and, he knew, it could only have been caused by some moving object.

Echlan had seen it too. Before Felix could report he heard the sergeant's voice.

'Unknown object approaching station on bearing three twenty-five. Distance about five miles.'

'Message received,' said a woman's voice. 'Switch to combat channel.'

A figure suddenly stood beside Felix and his helmet rang as the other made contact. It was Echlan, his voice distorted.

'There's a switch just before your chin. Knock it to the right. Got it?'

Felix found it and threw it with a thrust of his chin.

'Right. What was that for?'

'Limited radio-silence. Knock it back if there is an emergency. As from now we can talk to each other but you can't talk to control. Only I can do that. If I get killed or hurt then someone else will take over. Don't worry about anything until you're the last man alive.'

'You're joking.'

'Maybe. I hope so; but that thing out there may not be friendly and we can't afford to take any chances.'

Echlan left and Felix was conscious of movement. Suited figures melted into the rock, weapons at the ready. He suddenly felt very vulnerable.

'We should have had a couple of bazookas,' said a man grimly. 'These pop-guns won't even scratch their paint.'

'Shut up!' snapped Echlan. 'Use your eyes, not your mouth!'

There was strain in his voice and it was obvious why. If the station should be attacked the defenders wouldn't stand a chance and, if war had broken out on Earth, the station would be a prime target. It could even be the target selected to commence hostilities for the old conception of a formal declaration of war had been buried long ago.

Minutes dragged and the strain mounted. Felix lay tense, trying to ignore an itching place on his cheek, sweat stinging his eyes. From the distance, riding in a plume of dust, the mysterious vehicle came into sight.

'Hell!' A man was explosive with relief. 'It's the Yanks!'

'Hold it!' Echlan was a professional soldier. 'We can't be certain of that yet.'

'I recognise their runner, Sarge.'

'So they could be Yanks, but what of it? They could still be enemies. We stay alert until we know for certain.'

It was a cold, hard philosophy but the only one possible in the circumstances. For a while longer the tension continued then dissolved as Echlan received word from control.

'All right. The alert is over. It's General Klovis and his party.'

'I knew it,' said a disgusted voice. 'It had to be the Yanks. Trust them to knock the paint off their runner.'

'Some mechanic's going to get a rocket when Klovis finds out,' said another. 'I'd like to be there when he gets it.'

The banter continued. Interested in the strange vehicle Felix rose and, resting his weight on the edge of the crest, leaned forward as it approached the station. It was well-designed, he thought, perfectly adapted to crossing rugged ground at high speed and, aside from the bright patch of alloy where the paint had been scraped, would be almost invisible at any distance.

'If you're finished here, Felix we'll get down,' said Echlan. 'Have you done all you want to do?'

'Yes. The rest is up to the technicians.'

'Good. Let's get moving then.'

Felix stepped forward, the full weight of his body thrusting against his left foot, the one resting on the edge of the slope. Even as he moved he felt the support begin to yield and then, with horrifying abruptness, the entire edge fell away.

'Felix!'

For a moment he seemed to hang suspended then he began to fall. He was tilted forward and had a glimpse of a suited figure running towards him before his helmet smashed against the edge. There was a shattering impact and the viewport dissolved into a thousand tiny lines starring from a jagged opening. Air whined from the helmet followed by a spray of blood from the ruptured membranes of his nose.

Then he was falling, bouncing down the steep slope, rolling, blind and terrified to the ground almost a thousand feet below.

8

The scent was familiar; he knew who it was without needing to open his eyes.

'Hello, Gloria.'

He tried to move and winced at sudden pain. He was, he guessed, in a hospital bed and the smell of hospitals was in the air. They should, he thought, use different smells. Pine, say, or roses, or would floral scents remind the patients too much of the grave? Sandlewood then, and cedarwood and sweet white wine. Or perhaps the rich, rare spices of the East would scent away the butcher-association that was the heritage of hospitals. It was unfair they should be so maligned. Hospitals weren't like that now. They were simply places of healing and repair. Like garages; they were also places of repair. Did engines shudder at the smell of detergents, the sight of spanners?

He opened his eyes and guessed that he had been asleep or in a coma. Or perhaps she had sedated him; she was good at that.

'Hello, Gloria.'

'You said that,' she smiled. 'Five hours ago.'

'I did? Have you been here all this time?'

'No. Avril sat beside you. She insisted.'

'Where is she now?'

'Gone. She has her work to do.' Gloria took his pulse and nodded in satisfaction. 'Good. As far as I can see you are out of shock. Are you?'

'I don't know.' He frowned thoughtfully at the ceiling. 'I suppose I must be. Why am I still alive?'

'A combination of fortuitous circumstances commonly known as luck.'

'Good luck?'

'I didn't say that. Luck can be good or bad depending on the point of view. Yours, from your point of view, happened to be good.'

'I see.' He smiled. 'It seems that I was well-named, Gloria. Cats are popularly supposed to have nine lives, aren't they?'

'I shouldn't rely on it, Felix,' she said

solemnly. They both smiled.

'You smashed your helmet,' she said. 'At the same time loss of air caused a minor nasal haemorrhage — a nose bleed — and the blood pasted itself over most of the viewport and sealed it against further breakage. You rolled down the slope and fell into a patch of dust which broke your fall. You fell face-down so that the dust blocked the vent in the viewport. That, coupled with the blood, effectively saved you from asphyxiation.'

'Damage?'

'Bruises, sprains and shock. The shock has passed, the bruises and sprains are minor. You had better not go outside for a while just yet but otherwise you are in good working condition.'

He nodded and cautiously stretched himself. The earlier pains had vanished, probably medicated away and, aside from a slight stiffness, he felt quite well. Curiously he stared at the woman.

'Tell me,' he said, 'just what do you think are the chances of anyone living through the kind of accident I've just had?'

'I don't know. I am not a mathematician.'

'Perhaps not, but you must have some idea. Almost none, eh?'

'Almost. Why?'

'I am a curious man, Gloria. Friends have told me it's my biggest failing. Do I need another reason?'

'I suppose not. You . . .'

She broke off as the intercom hummed into life. It was a signal-call, he noted, which made her one of the few people to be so summoned.

'Yes?'

'The Director would like to see you in his office,' said the woman in control. 'Are you available?'

'Yes. I will be along in a few minutes.' She released the button and stood for a moment, frowning in thought.

'Trouble, Gloria?'

'What a stupid question!' She came to a decision. 'I want you to stay in bed while I've gone. Avril will probably drop in to see you later so you may as well wait for her. I'll give you something to make you sleep until she arrives.'

105

'More pills, Gloria?'

'Take it.' It was small, round and of a vivid blue. 'Hurry,' she said impatiently. 'It will clear up the last vestiges of shock.'

He sighed, took the pill and putting it into his mouth made hard work of swallowing.

'Water!'

'Here.' She handed him a cup. 'Swallowed it? Good. Settle down now and don't get out of bed.'

He smiled as she bustled about the ward, letting his eyes close and breathing shallowly as if asleep. He heard her walk towards him and rolled up his eyes. The precaution was unnecessary, she did not lift an eyelid.

Only when he was certain she had gone did he sit up and spit the dissolving pill into his hand.

The ward was small, six beds together with an oxygen apparatus, some cabinets of drugs and instruments and an X-ray machine. A door led, he supposed, to an operating theatre and another opened into a small office containing filing cabinets and medical records.

Aside from himself the ward was empty. Slipping from the bed he crossed to the door, opened it a crack and saw the back of a guard. Softly he closed the panel. Crossing to the other door he opened it and saw, as he had expected, an operating table in the centre of the room. He stood, running his eyes over the appointments of the theatre and wondered if Gloria had personally selected her equipment. If so she had done a superb job. He doubted if better was to be found in even the most modern hospital.

Stepping into the theatre he glanced to his left and saw the other man.

'Seldon!' Felix stared at the face, so familiar from photographs. 'Seldon! What the hell are you doing in here?'

'What . . . ?' Heavy eyelids opened and revealed eyes of murky brown. 'What . . . '

He was, Felix thought, still half-asleep or under the influence of drugs. He was in an odd position, certainly not in a bed but rather as if he sat on a chair. A sheet was wrapped around his neck and covered the rest. His face, though much thinner, had a healthy colour and he didn't seem to be ill.

'Seldon! Wake up!' Felix gently squeezed the man's cheeks, pursing his mouth so that his lips protruded like those of a gasping fish. It was a means to wake a person without causing shock or alarm and without knowing more of the man's condition he dared not be too rough.

'What . . . don't do that!' His voice was thin but without weakness. 'Who are you?'

'A friend.' Felix lowered his voice. 'Do you know the sum total of the combination of Sir Joshua's safe?'

'I do.' Seldon mentioned it. 'Did he send you?'

'Yes.' Felix carefully closed the operating theatre's door and returned to the other man. He was conscious of a rising excitement; this man could tell him all he had to know.

The government trusted no one. They had staffed the station with selected personnel but among them they had put one who had orders to send secret reports direct to Whitehall. That man was Seldon.

He was the cause of Felix having been sent to the moon.

'What happened,' said Felix. 'You haven't sent any reports for over six months and the ones before that showed you were worried about something. What was it?'

'Nothing.' Seldon moistened his lips with the tip of his tongue. 'Water,' he said. 'Get me some water. You'll find a cup over by the washing bowl.'

The cup was of the type used to give liquids to immobile patients. It had a cover and a spout through which they could drink. Felix filled it and carried it back to Seldon.

'Just a little,' he said. 'Just enough to wet my lips . . . they get so dry.'

'How badly are you hurt?'

'Pretty bad. It was an accident . . . but never mind that now. What is Sir Joshua worried about?'

'Don't you know?' Felix felt a sudden annoyance. 'According to you something was going seriously wrong up here. You said that you were worried and suspected enemy agents. Well?'

'I don't know . . . it's hard to remember.'

'How do you mean? Have you been drugged? I don't mean medically.'

'No, I don't think so.'

'Then, damn it, let's get to business! I'm tired of working in the dark and there isn't time if what you hinted is true. Are there enemy agents in the station?'

'I thought there might be.'

'Who? Have you any suspicions?'

'Leaver.'

'Leaver. Anyone else?'

'I don't know. I . . . Can I have another drink?'

Felix restrained his impatience as he moistened the other's mouth. He was obviously ill, perhaps seriously so even if he didn't look it, and a little vagueness was to be expected.

'Try and think,' he urged. 'You know how serious this is. You reported that you were unhappy at the way things were going at the station. What did you mean by that?'

'Odd things.' Seldon's eyes were clear now. 'You know how it is when you sense that something isn't quite as it should be but just can't put your finger on it. The Eyrie for example, why go to all that trouble to provide a view?'

'And?'

'The breakdown of demarcation among the personnel.'

'And?'

'I don't know. A lot of little things. A mental attitude, perhaps. It made me uneasy.'

'Are you still uneasy?'

'No.'

'Why not?'

'How can I answer that? I just don't feel concerned any more.' Oddly the man laughed, it had a peculiarly empty sound. Felix bit his lip, this was getting him nowhere.

'Listen,' he said urgently. 'I know that you've been badly hurt but please try and concentrate. We may not have another chance to talk alone. Have you any reason to suspect that there is any large-scale subversion here?'

'How could there be?'

'I'm asking the questions!'

'I don't know. At one time I think I feared that as a possibility but I simply couldn't see how it could come about. I mean, there was no propaganda, no insidious incentive to betray our trust.'

'Yet you suspected it?'

'At one time, yes.'

'But you were never able to obtain proof?'

'No.'

'I see.' Felix reverted to an earlier statement. 'You said that you don't feel concerned about it any more. Do you mean that you don't give a damn what happens to the station?'

'Of course not. I mean that it doesn't worry me now as it did.' Seldon laughed again. 'In fact very few things worry me now. Perhaps because I am powerless to do anything about it no matter what may happen.' He paused. 'I've not been very much help to you, have I?'

'No.' Felix was honest.

'I'm sorry, but you must remember that, in my position, I had to suspect everything. It wasn't for me to arrive at a conclusion but only to report the facts as

I saw them and add a general impression. I was disturbed and said so. That impression could have been quite wrong.'

'I don't think it was,' said Felix. 'Is that all you can tell me?'

'I'm afraid so. You must realise that I have not been mobile for some time now. You probably have a clearer picture of the establishment than I have and there is always the possibility that I was too prone to caution. Even so, that was hardly a fault.'

Seldon hadn't been at fault, thought Felix bleakly. His position had been that of a watchman in a munitions factory who suspects the presence of matches and had sent for an inspector to find them before the explosion. Felix was the inspector.

'I'm going to have a look round,' he told Seldon. 'Is there anything you want?'

'A sip of water, please.'

Felix moistened his lips, wondering why the man didn't drink and have done with it. He was a little curious about Seldon's injuries. He seemed alert enough, his eyes were bright and his skin clear, but he couldn't even move his head let alone any other part of his body.

'Thank you.'

'I'll leave you now.' Felix returned the cup as he had found it. 'There is no need to tell you that this talk was confidential. I would rather no one knew that I have seen you.'

'I understand.'

★　★　★

Gloria was a neat woman and kept her office as neat as herself. Her records were each filed in their correct place and told her what she or any other doctor would want to know about the personnel of the station. Felix was not a doctor even though he knew quite a lot about medicine but he did know something of women. He smiled as an open drawer revealed a small bust of Macdonald. It had been carved from some soft stone, probably a fragment from one of the great 'rays' which streamed from Tycho, and it was an extremely good likeness.

'So,' he said softly to himself as he

looked at it. 'Our precise lady sawbones is a true woman at heart after all.'

He replaced the bust and continued his search, not knowing just what he was looking for but knowing that it would register if he found it. He leafed through official papers, directives from Whitehall, files, records and a mass of medical literature of an obviously American origin. That, he assumed, had come from the American base. He carefully read several sheets of handwriting and found they were poetry and very good poetry indeed. Finally he picked up the hospital casualty book.

It was, he found, a very comprehensive record. It dated from the first days of the establishment to the present time and he smiled at the last entry, his own.

Dec. 13th. 22.10 hrs. Larsen Felix. Fall from outside cliff approx. 1,000 ft. Viewport of helmet shattered at commencement of fall. Minor injuries.

Terse, he thought, a bald statement which was probably expanded in the correct file together with what medication she had seen fit to give him. He looked at an earlier entry.

Dec. 10th. 02.34 hrs. Maynard Colin. Attempted suicide. Cartridge misfired. Psychic shock.

So she had guessed or Maynard had told her, it made no difference. But, from what he had gathered from Echlan, Maynard had returned to duty, the incident was closed and the whole thing remained an official mystery. In that case either Gloria had not bothered to report the incident to either Crombie or Macdonald or . . .

He stood very still, the book in his hands, the peculiar impression that he hovered on the verge of an important discovery beating in his mind.

. . . or she had reported it and neither of them had considered it to be important enough to worry about. And she must have reported it. The records must be subject to examination and, if she had wanted to cover the incident then why record it at all?

Felix sighed, his eyes thoughtful. No military commander in his experience would dare to overlook a thing like the attempted suicide of one of his men. No establishment dealing in wholesale death would dare to allow a psychotic personality with suicidal tendencies to run loose. Not when, driven by the death wish, he could destroy himself and the entire installation with him. Such a thing simply wouldn't happen when once it was brought to the notice of the authorities.

Not unless it was of so common an occurrence that it was regarded as normal behaviour.

Hastily he began to riffle through the book then snapped it shut at the sound of voices from beyond the guarded door. Quickly he replaced it, took a fast look around the office to make certain that everything was as he had found it, and reached the bed just as the door began to swing open. Eyes closed, breathing shallow, he simulated sleep as footsteps crossed the room towards him.

A hand touched his forehead and gently stroked his hair. It was very soft, very cool, and very feminine. It didn't belong to Gloria.

'Poor Felix.' Avril's voice held a tone he hadn't heard before. 'Why do I have to love you so much?'

He sighed and slowly opened his eyes, smiling up into her face poised above his own.

'Hello, Angel.'

'You're not dead, silly.'

'Does that make a difference?'

It was natural to kiss but he was startled by the sharp emotion the touch of her lips brought to sudden life. He covered it with an artificial yawn and sat up in the bed.

'Have you been here long?'

'Guess?'

'An hour?' He shook his head. 'No, I can't guess. Have you?'

'No.'

He yawned again and rubbed his eyes, wondering just how strong that blue pill had been. Not very strong, probably, Gloria had known that Avril was coming for him, but he had to play it safe.

'Damn that woman and her pills! I feel worn out.'

'She means well.'

'Maybe, but as far as I'm concerned

she's just a cold-blooded pill-pusher with a fluoroscope for a heart.' He looked down at his near-nakedness. 'This is beginning to get a habit. Now where did she put my coverall?'

Avril found it hanging in a cupboard and held it while he laved his face and neck at the sink. He made no effort to be curious about what was behind the closed door and hoped that he was staying in character.

'Felix!' Avril looked at him, an odd expression in her eyes.

'Yes?'

'Felix, when you were falling, from that cliff, I mean, what did you think about?'

'Think?' He frowned, surprised at her question, then shrugged. 'I can't remember. I was as scared as hell, I know that.'

'Nothing else?'

'Yes,' he said slowly. 'There was, now I come to think about it. I felt anger and regret. Anger at having been so foolish as to stand so near the edge and regret at . . . '

' . . . at lost opportunities?'

'I can't remember. Are we going to eat

or do I have to stay here until Gloria returns?'

'She's busy at the moment. I suppose you can leave now and we can eat together.' She slipped her arm through his. 'Did you, Felix?'

'Did I what?'

'Regret lost opportunities?'

'Not exactly. I regretted not having stayed on Earth when I had the chance.'

He lied and he hoped she didn't know it. He had suffered regret as he fell and he had thought of a particular person with reference to that emotion. He had thought of Avril and he knew why.

It was a pity that he couldn't trust her but he couldn't trust her or anyone now. Especially not now. Not since he had learned that Seldon was useless and that he was totally on his own.

9

'Well, folks!' General Klovis raised his glass. 'Here's to our continued understanding!'

Ten people drank the toast with various degrees of appreciation. Gloria made a face as she swallowed the spirit and Macdonald smiled at her.

'Just go through the motions,' he whispered. 'You don't have to drink the stuff.'

'I know but I need it. How much longer is this going on?'

'Not too long, I hope.' He hesitated. 'Is everything all right?'

'Yes.'

'Good. Be gracious now, we have to be polite.'

Lord Severn needed no such urging. He smiled as he set down his glass. 'Surely, General, there is no fear that we shall ever be other than the best of friends?' He neither waited for nor expected an answer. 'Rather good bourbon this.'

'Each man to his taste,' said Macdonald evenly. He sipped at his glass. 'Imported, General?'

'Good grief, no!' Klovis chuckled as he refilled the glasses from the plastic bottle. 'We aren't that rich, Sir Ian. No. We have an old moonshiner from Kentucky at the base.' He raised his glass for a second toast. 'Here's to closer co-operation!'

'In which way, General!' Macdonald stood, the glass in his hand, his eyes very direct as they stared at the American. Klovis shrugged.

'In every way. We, you and us, are partners all along the line.'

'Agreed. But closer co-operation would mean that we are no longer partners.'

'Now I don't get that.' Klovis gestured towards the members of the Commission. 'I feel, and I think that I'm not alone, that we could be a great deal closer than we are. Defence, for one thing. I mean no insult, Director, but I could take this base any time I wanted. And if I could do it then so could the Reds.'

'I see.' Macdonald set down his glass. 'Major Crombie!'

'Yes, Sir Ian.'

'If we were attacked, by any foreign force, what would you do?'

'Destroy the station.'

'Utterly?'

'To the last man and woman.' Crombie's eyes were as hard as Macdonald's. The Director smiled.

'You see, General Klovis? If any strong force tried to capture this station they would win only a semi-molten patch in the ground.' Macdonald raised his glass. 'Now, with your permission, General Klovis, I would like to propose a toast.'

'Sure. Go right ahead.'

'To freedom — in the truest sense of the word!'

They drank, Klovis admiring the Director's spirit and feeling a little sorry for him. He had made his point but only just.

Klovis found it all interesting. It had been a stroke of luck finding the visitors at the station and it hadn't been difficult to figure just why they were there. Watts had talked and so had Meeson, business was international and defence was so integrated that neither of them had wanted to risk being thought unco-operative. Macdonald, though he might not know it, was way out on a limb.

It was time to drop his bombshell.

'I don't believe it!' Crombie was emphatic. 'It simply isn't possible!'

'It's a fact.' Rasch spread out his graphs and figures. 'These can't lie, Major. I tell you that someone in this station is sending out messages and we can guess to whom!'

It had shaken them, Klovis could see that. Unconsciously he unwrapped a cigar, stuck it in his mouth and then remembered that there was no smoking on the station. He sucked at the unlit cylinder as he tried to read their faces.

He had been cautious. Only the Major, Sir Ian, General Watts and himself together with Rasch were in the inner room. The rest of the Commission together with the doctor had been left outside. For Security reasons if for no other this thing had to be classified as restricted information. But Watts, he guessed, would tell Lord Severn and that would mean a tightening of the screw.

'I don't like to keep playing the same tune, Sir Ian,' he said smoothly, 'but it's a matter of manpower. You simply can't watch everyone all the time and a spy wouldn't have a hard job escaping discovery, especially if he's using some new gadget which doesn't register on your instruments.'

'If there is a spy. Personally I doubt that very much.'

'Do you doubt Rasch's figures?'

'Yes.'

'Come again, Sir Ian?'

'I think you understood me, General Klovis.' The Director was very precise. 'Shall we have some plain speaking?'

'Shoot.'

'For a long time now your government has wanted control of this station. This could be a means of bringing pressure to bear. If there is a spy here, as you say, then obviously he must be caught. You claim that we cannot clean our own house. I disagree.'

'The facts prove otherwise, Sir Ian.' He was, thought Klovis, a fighting devil and he admired him for it, but he was waging a losing battle.

'No, General Klovis, they do not. These figures,' Macdonald flipped the papers with the tip of a finger, 'what do they prove? As far as I am concerned they prove nothing at all. You claim to have received them and taken bearings which lead to this base. Do I have to remind you that, on the moon, radio operates on line-of-sight? How, then, could you have obtained bearings?'

'Well, Rasch?' Klovis turned to the captain. Macdonald was smart, he hadn't thought of that. His eyes warned the captain that he had better have a good explanation.

'They are not signals on the electro-magnetic spectrum,' said Rasch. 'They obviously do not operate under the same restrictions.'

'A neat explanation.' Macdonald glanced at General Watts then back to Rasch. 'If they are not radio signals then how do you know they are messages?'

'I've explained that.'

'Yes, so you have, if your explanation is the correct one. But couldn't they be signals emanating from the sun? Even from Earth? A freak transmission, perhaps?'

'No.'

'You seem very confident?'

'I am.' Rasch, Klovis saw, was getting rattled. 'Why do you refuse to accept the obvious?'

'Is it obvious?' Macdonald shrugged. 'General Watts? Is it so obvious to you?'

'I'm not a scientist,' said the General slowly, 'but I can see your point, Sir Ian. I take it that you monitor the station?'

'Constantly.'

'Spot searches?'

'At regular intervals.' Crombie joined in the argument. 'Really, General Watts, this accusation is ridiculously far-fetched.'

'Perhaps, Major, but we can take no chances.' Watts, Klovis could see, was undecided. As a visitor he had no real power in the station and he hesitated to give Macdonald an order which could result in an outright refusal. The Director broke the impasse.

'There is a simple way out of all this,' he said evenly. 'Your detecting instrument, Captain Rasch, is portable and . . .'

'I didn't say that, Sir Ian,' said Rasch and Klovis inwardly cursed the man for a fool. Macdonald looked surprised.

'But you took bearings! You could only have done that by taking readings from several widely separated points. You had to carry your detectors so they must be portable.'

'Yes . . . I suppose they are.'

'Do you have one in the runner?'

'Yes . . . that is, no. I . . . '

'We have one,' sighed Klovis. Rasch would never make a diplomat or anything else, he was too transparent.

'Good.' Macdonald looked pleased and, thought Klovis sourly, he had reason to be. 'Then the whole thing is simple. You loan us your detector and, if we register any overt signalling, we can take steps to discover who is responsible.' He smiled at the discomfited Klovis. 'So easy when you put your mind to it, isn't it General?'

'Yeah. Yeah I guess it is.'

'Agreed, General Watts?'

'It seems an excellent idea to me, Sir Ian.' Watts was expansive at having escaped the necessity of making an awkward decision. 'That's settled then, eh, Klovis?'

He had no choice but to agree.

10

The rat was a prime, healthy specimen of the tame white variety so beloved by schoolboys and so detested by fond female parents. Ottoway held it in gloved hands, stroking the short fur as he held it in plain view.

'Gentlemen, please regard this animal.'

The members of the Commission stirred on their chairs and Macdonald hoped the bio-physicist wasn't going to act the fool. They wanted a demonstration, not a lecture, but there was nothing he could do but hope that Ottoway would get the unpleasant business over as quickly as he could.

'A rat,' said Ottoway evenly, 'is, biologically speaking, very much like a man. They are relatively intelligent, relatively small and very easy to breed. They make ideal laboratory specimens. Remember that what affects a rat will affect a man. Think of this animal as being a man.'

He nodded to Jeff who came forward with a plastic box. Ottoway put the rat in the box and closed the lid, watching as the animal raced around the enclosure, sharp nose twitching at the transparent barrier.

'I would like to talk about biological warfare for a moment,' continued Ottoway. He smiled at the Director. 'Don't be afraid that I am going to preach, that isn't my job, but it would help if you understood the problem from the ground up, so to speak. Now, as you all know, plagues like smallpox, typhoid, cholera and the bubonic plague of the Middle Ages are extremely virulent but they are not total in their destruction-potential. Some affected people recover. Some simply do not succumb and, of course, vaccines and innoculations can now give immunity.'

'I think we are all aware of that, Ottoway,' said General Watts impatiently.

'I am pleased to hear it, General.' Ottoway remained bland. 'But if I may continue — ?'

'Go on,' said Connor. 'I find this

extremely interesting.'

'Thank you.' Ottoway paused as if waiting for further comments then plunged ahead.

'I don't want to bore you, gentlemen, so I will summarise. A military biological weapon must have certain capabilities. It must remain virulent over long periods of storage. It must be easily disseminated and quickly propagated. The death-rate of victims should be one hundred per cent and there should be no obvious antibiotic. By this I mean that the weapon itself should not serve to fashion its own vaccine as, for example, in the case of smallpox.'

'But there surely must be some form of protection,' said Connor. 'Otherwise it would be a double-edged weapon. We would suffer as much as the enemy.'

'Exactly.' Ottoway rested his hand on the case, the movement disturbing the rat who froze in one corner, its tiny ruby eyes reflecting the lights with startling brilliance.

'That has always been a major problem, Mr. Connor, and an obvious one. We have developed virus diseases against which the bubonic plagues are as relatively harmless as a common cold — but once released they will devastate both sides. Also, by their very nature, they cannot be guaranteed one hundred per cent fatal or effective.'

Connor nodded, deep lines of thought creasing his forehead, and Macdonald wondered if he were calculating the effect of such a holocaust on the financial system of the capitalist countries. He shrugged, knowing that he was possibly being unfair, and listened to what Ottoway was saying.

' . . . nerve gases,' said the bio-physicist. 'They are effective and quite lethal but they are not self-propagating. The problem then, as we saw it, was to develop something of a similar nature but which would contain all the desired attributes of the ideal weapon. We have succeeded.'

He was, thought Macdonald, quite a showman when he set himself out to be.

★   ★   ★

There was an inlet valve on the side of the case in which the rat crouched in terrified immobility. Jeff opened a cabinet, took out a small container and passed it to Ottoway. He poised it in his hand.

'The contents of this vial,' he said with unconscious dramatic effect, 'if released in the air of this room, would kill every living thing in the station within five minutes.'

He screwed it to the inlet valve of the case and rested his fingers on the release screw.

'The virus it contains was one developed from nucleic acids and is quite artificial. It does not occur in nature. It is anaerobic, that is it can live without free oxygen, and has still remained virulent after being subjected to immersion in liquid helium and boiled in pressurised steam. It fulfils all the requirements of the perfect biological weapon. Now watch as I show you how it works.'

Ottoway twisted the screw and the members of the Commission tensed, leaning forward on their chairs. Macdonald did not tense, he had seen this before, but he felt a little sick. It was never pleasant to see a helpless creature die.

A faint spray came from the vial, immediately dissipating into the air of the case. For a few seconds nothing happened and then, quite suddenly, the rat slumped. It was not dead, the eyes still shone with life, but it looked as if paralysed.

The nose twitched once, the tail stirred a little and then fell like a limp piece of string. Suddenly the light went from the tiny ruby eyes.

'Fifteen seconds,' said Ottoway. 'I know that you didn't time it, gentlemen, but you can take my word for it. A man would take a little longer.'

'Incredible!' Connor was, Macdonald noticed, sweating and his eyes held a horrified expression. 'Did it suffer?'

'Of course it didn't.' Prentice was quick to soothe the other's fears. 'It just fell asleep. Isn't that right, Ottoway?'

'Not exactly. The virus attacked the acetylchline in the creature's body.' Ottoway looked down at the case. 'To be able to move, your brain has to send a message along the nerves to the appropriate muscles. The nerves are not continuous threads of tissue. They are, if you like, more like a row of bricks each almost, but not quite, touching the other. Acetylchline is the stuff between the segments of nervous tissue that enables the electrical stimulus to progress over the minute gaps. Ordinary nerve gases affect this message-carrying capacity to some extent but the virus you have just seen at work utterly destroys it.

'A person attacked by the virus becomes paralysed, a helpless brain locked in unresponsive flesh. For a short while, life, that is consciousness, will continue and then death provides a welcome relief. There is no cure, no natural resistance, no hope of survival once attacked. The death-rate is one hundred per cent. Our calculations have shown that one single container of the virus, released in any large town, will totally destroy every inhabitant of that town within three hours. By selected dissemination it is possible literally to wipe out all life, and I mean all life, animal as well as human, from the entire globe within three days.'

'I don't believe it!' General Watts was incredulous. Ottoway shrugged.

'It's a fact, General. When the very atmosphere becomes contaminated and every victim is a source of continual infection then the end is inevitable. The virus will only become dormant when there is nothing on which it can breed.'

'But — '

'Why are you so incredulous?' Ottoway was impatient. 'After all, the fallout from present atomic weapons can do the job just as thoroughly as this virus and with exactly the same end-result. Both will lead to the utter annihilation of every living thing on earth.'

'But not if we have an antibiotic,' said Prentice shrewdly.

Ottoway looked at the Director.

'We have protection?' Prentice was sharp. Macdonald slowly shook his head.

'No,' he said grimly. 'That is why the virus must never leave this station.'

They did not smoke at the station.

Economics, not ethics had dictated the custom, tobacco was an unessential luxury and the air pollution was something to be avoided when slender resources were already strained to the limit, but the members of the Commission were beyond ethical consideration.

Even so Macdonald had insisted that they restrict their indulgence to a special room he had placed at their disposal for private discussion and relaxation.

'Well, gentlemen.' Lord Severn carefully lit a cigar, noting with regret that it was the last but one of the few which weight-limitations had permitted him to carry in his personal baggage. 'I have no desire to hurry you, of course, but we can hardly stay here indefinitely. If you are all quite certain that you have satisfied yourselves . . . ?'

He let the question hang in the air, busy with his Havana, too subtle to commit himself to any course of action until he knew the direction of the popular wind.

'I've seen enough.' General Watts was terse and to the point.

'Me too.' Meeson echoed the General and Prentice made a murmur of agreement. Connor hesitated.

'Well,' he said. 'I'd like to be sure on one or two points.'

'Such as?' Prentice wanted to get back to his firm and suspected that Connor didn't share his reasons for haste. His tone betrayed his impatience and Connor bridled. Lord Severn noticed it and smoothly the old diplomat healed the breach.

'We are here to do a task of investigation for Her Majesty's Government,' he said silkily. 'It is our duty to carry out our Commission as best we may. However, I feel that we should try to avoid putting any extra burden on the Director. Do you agree, Connor?'

Put like that Connor had no choice. If he insisted then he would be a nuisance to the Director and to the rest of the Commission. He decided not to be a nuisance. Lord Severn smiled his appreciation.

'Good. Now, perhaps, if I may make a suggestion?'

Their agreement was unanimous.

'Well, I was thinking that we could spend the rest of our time here in arriving at some informal agreement as to our findings.' His smile was bland. 'The Prime Minister, I know for a fact, would appreciate an early report.'

'I know what is obvious enough,' snapped General Watts. 'The defences of this place are ludicrous. Any attempt at defence would be futile. Crombie's a good man but you know what these die-hards are. In this day and age you've got to face facts and forget sentimental nonsense. Klovis had a good point when he said that we needed his help, not when we are attacked, but here waiting for any attack to come.'

'Wouldn't that mean the station becoming just another part of the American defence zone?' Connor was thoughtful. 'I don't think that I wholly agree with that idea.'

'Would you rather the Reds get their hands on what you've seen in action?' Watts gestured in the general direction of the laboratories. 'You saw what it did to that rat. Do you want to see the same thing happen to the Western world?'

'Of course not. But Crombie promised that he would destroy the station rather than let that happen.'

'Yes — if he could.' The General was grim. 'But suppose he didn't get the chance? The station could be sabotaged, enemy agents spring a surprise attack, anything. No, I don't think we should run any unessential risk.'

'Sir Ian would never permit the Americans to establish a garrison here,' said Meeson thoughtfully.

'Then Sir Ian would have to be replaced!'

'Is that fair?'

'Gentlemen!' Lord Severn gestured with his cigar. 'Let us be calm about this. Sir Ian has been here for over seven years and that is a long time for any man to be away from home. It would be a kindness to relieve him of such responsibility. There would be rewards, a peerage certainly, perhaps even a place in the diplomatic corps. Do not let your judgement be influenced by the thought of any disgrace. Sir Ian has nothing to fear on that score.'

'Maybe not.' Watts irritably crushed out his cigarette. He was in a dilemma. Klovis' suspicion of a spy operating within the station was a forceful argument but one he couldn't use. While he sat glowering at the smouldering butt Prentice came to his assistance.

'What Sir Ian wants and what he doesn't want is beside the point,' he said primly. 'Surely it is the government which makes decisions on this level. I agree with General Watts. I think the station should be under American protection. If this is difficult under the present Director then he should be replaced by a man with a more co-operative attitude.'

'Could you . . . ' Lord Severn broke off with a frown as the intercom hummed a signal. 'Confound those boxes!' He waited impatiently until the signal cut into silence. 'Could you finalise that, Prentice?'

'Certainly, Lord Severn. I think the Director should be replaced and I shall so recommend.'

'Thank you. Meeson?'

'I am against the suggestion.'

'I see. General Watts, you I take it are in agreement. Connor?'

'I suppose it's for the best.'

'Yes, I think that it is.' Now that he knew the will of the majority Lord Severn had no hesitation. 'I must admit that my feelings in the matter are the same. It is no secret that, for some time now, the government has been embarrassed by this problem. A full scale defence programme of the station at this time would be a heavy burden on the expenditure and the opposition would be quick to make capital of the matter. On the other hand it is essential that we show our implicit trust and confidence in our allies and . . . '

He broke off as an attention signal hummed from the intercom.

'Really. This is too much!'

Impatiently he waited for the sound to cease.

11

Felix hefted his pick, drove it into rock with a surge of shoulder and back muscles, jerked it free with a shower of stone and paused to wipe the sweat from his forehead.

'If this is recreation,' he said feelingly, 'then give me the salt mines.'

'You're joking.' His companion, a stocky West Indian, grinned as he picked up a boulder that would have weighed half a ton back on his native island. 'Who wants salt?'

'I do.' Felix looked at his streaming palm. 'The way I'm sweating I'll be suffering from cramp before I know it.' He wasn't serious and the others of the working party knew it. But he was, to his surprise, in poor physical condition as aching muscles and quick fatigue had shown.

Stones flew, then he staggered as his foot trod on a loose shard, the pick glancing from the rock face, swinging wildly towards the man at his side.

'Steady!' Toni gripped his arm. 'There's no sense in overdoing it. We don't have to dig our way through the mountain.'

'What are we doing, anyway?'

'Extending the living quarters, not that it matters. We do it for exercise, remember?'

Felix nodded, still feeling the cold touch of fear that had gripped him when the pick had swung towards the other. It had been sheer chance that Toni had moved at that exact moment. If he hadn't the pick would have split his skull.

'I've had enough.' He flung down the tool. 'I need a shower and the biggest synthetic steak the station can produce. Is it all right if I quit now?'

'Sure.' Toni winked. 'Avril's on kitchen duty so I guess you'll get your steak. Maybe she could find one for me too, eh?'

His rich, understanding laugh rolled from the workings as Felix left the chamber.

★　★　★

145

He had his shower and steak and then wandered over the station feeling at a loss. He felt tense and irritable like a man who has tackled too big a problem and isn't certain just how to start. Felix had never been trained in counter-espionage, his field was the far more subtle workings of the human mind and, while he could thread his way through a maze of complex motivations, yet he lacked the hunter-instinct which was essential to those seeking human quarry.

If only Seldon had been able to help.

That, he realised, was the trouble. Subconsciously he had been relying on the other man, seeing in himself an impartial observer who could correlate the data supplied by the agent. But Seldon was a helpless invalid, his information vague and out of date. If Felix was to discover what was wrong with the station he had to do it on his own.

And there was something wrong.

He had sensed it in a dozen little ways. Small things in themselves but adding up to one big question mark. It wasn't anything as clear-cut as sabotage and it wasn't the instinctive secrecy of those who suspect a spy in their midst. It was, rather, an attitude of mind and all the more vague because of that.

He paused before one of the doors, not surprised when it swung open. Jeff Carter stepped through the portal.

'Felix!' His smile was genuine. 'Long time no see.'

'I've been busy,' explained Felix. 'Working outside and the rest of it. How are things with the lab?'

'Abic?' Jeff shrugged. 'Nothing new, but then what did you expect? Scientific discoveries take time.' He began to laugh. 'Did you hear about Bob Howard's new job?'

'No.'

'You didn't?' Jeff hesitated, then came to a decision. 'I suppose the Yanks want it kept secret but you're in the same line so what's the difference? Anyway, you can't keep things quiet in the station.'

That, thought Felix sourly, was nothing but the truth.

'They've dreamed up a detector, or at

least Rasch and his staff did.'

Felix waited.

'Anyway,' Jeff continued, 'Klovis thought that someone in the station was signalling outside. So he saw Sir Ian and Rasch trained Bob how to use his gadget. It's a neat device, I'll give it that, but they got hold of the wrong end of the stick when they thought we had a spy in here.'

He looked up as the intercom began to call his name. He was wanted in the electronics laboratory. He frowned.

'The trouble with Bob is that he's too impatient,' said Jeff. 'Tell you what, Felix, why not come along with me? You'll be interested.'

Felix doubted it but he had no choice, not if he was to stay in his assumed character. And it would be a good idea to learn as much as he could about everything.

Bob looked up as they entered his domain. He sat at a table, a complex apparatus before him, the only part of which Felix recognised was a stylo tracing a line on graph paper.

'Hi, Jeff! Felix!'

'What's the hurry,' said Jeff. 'Did you have to page me twice?'

'I want to clear up something so that I can do some real work,' said Bob. He gestured towards the apparatus. 'What do you think of Rasch's detector?' he said to Felix.

'It looks rough.'

'Bread-board assemblies usually do,' said Bob drily. 'What do you make of it?'

It was something that could have been dreamed up by Heath Robinson, a conglomeration of parts which, to Felix, had neither reason nor purpose. He recognised a coil, a vernier dial, a permanent magnet and what could only be an amplifier. Two small Jurgens batteries obviously provided power. Without any real knowledge he could only bluff.

'What's it supposed to do?'

'According to Rasch it detects sentient life, among other things.' Bob leaned forward and threw a small switch. The roll of graph paper began to unwind, the stylo tracing a thin, blue line. The graph paper, Felix noted, was time-marked.

'Interesting.'

'It's more than that.' Bob pointed to some of the parts. 'Two transistors, a quartz crystal, a sheet of iron and another of copper. Add the magnet, coil and dial and that's the lot. The amplifier is standard. Well?'

He was waiting, Felix knew, for his 'professional' opinion.

'There are the connecting wires, of course.' He bent over the machine and then remembered where he had seen something like it once before. It had been at an exhibition of inexpicable phenomena, presented more as a scientific joke than for any serious purpose, and among the exhibits had been what were known as psionic machines.

'It shouldn't work,' he said firmly. 'The parts make no sense taken separately but, if it does something, then it must be because of their relationship with one another. It does work?'

'It works,' said Bob disgustedly. 'It shouldn't but it does. At least it registers something. Rasch claimed that it detected signals similar to human thought but much stronger and far more variable.' He glanced at Jeff. 'That's why I wanted to see you.'

'How can I help?'

'Rasch didn't know what we know. He received signals far too strong to have been emitted by a human mind and, naturally, suspected the worst. But I don't think we have a mysterious spy lurking in the station sending out our secrets by means of a superior form of radio. I've been checking this thing and if those signals make any sense then the spy, if there is one, is using a code that bears no relation to any form of communication that I've ever heard of.'

'Can you be certain of that?' Felix was interested. Bob nodded.

'Yes. I . . . ' He broke off as the intercom hummed into life.

'Attention all personnel! The Royal Commission is about to leave. Take-off will be relayed to all screens.'

'At last!' Bob rose and crossed to a screen. It flared to life as he turned a switch and he grinned at Felix's expression.

'What's the use of having an electronics laboratory if you don't make use of it? We can watch in comfort from here.'

★   ★   ★

It came, Felix suspected, under the heading of entertainment and he admired the Director for his foresight in his practice of keeping the station informed of all events which had the slightest effect on their welfare. Knowledge killed rumour and, with recreation facilities limited, it was wise to take every advantage of anything to break the monotony. He guessed that every landing and take-off was so televised.

'They're taking their time,' said Jeff as the screen showed only the bare terrain and the waiting rocket. 'Do we have to look at this?'

'Why not?' Bob was casual. 'It's not every day we get the chance to wave a high-priced bunch of baskets goodbye.'

'To hell with them!' Jeff was savage. Felix changed the subject.

'You were talking about the signals,' he

reminded Bob. 'Why are you so certain they aren't a message?'

'Any signal which carries a message must have some form of repetition no matter how random the pattern may appear. You can take a message, scramble it, add irrelevancies, increase background noise and turn it this way to Sunday but, buried in the mess, you still have a message. You may not know what that message is but you can recognise it — especially if it falls into the field of human communication.'

He gestured to the slowly revolving roll of graph paper.

'This has no repetition at all. It's too variable both in frequency and intensity. I've been running it since Rasch left, far longer than necessary to establish any sort of pattern, and there just isn't one to establish.'

'Have you tried acceleration? Resonance? Reverse amplification?'

'Naturally.' Bob sounded surprised at the question.

'Sorry,' Felix apologised. 'I shouldn't try to teach you your job.'

'No, you shouldn't.'

There was a quiet irony in the other's tone and Felix wondered just how he had betrayed himself. Not that it mattered too much, he had never claimed to be an expert, but it was annoying.

'Does the Major know about this?'

'Not yet. I wanted to check with Jeff before I broke the good news. Anyway, he's too busy seeing off the Commission.' Bob glanced at the screen. 'There they go.'

Stark in the external sunlight the crawler lumbered like a primeval monster towards the slender shaft of the rocket ship.

'Ten minutes and they'll be heading for home.' Jeff made a harsh sound deep in his throat. 'Why the hell couldn't they have stayed there in the first place?'

'I take it that you don't like our late visitors?'

'I hate their guts!' Jeff glared at Felix as if he included him with the Commission. 'Penny-pinching politicians without the sense to see that they're cutting their own throats. That would be fine but the swine intend to cut ours at the same time. It's pompous, big-mouthed fools like those who have put the world in the state it's in. And you ask if I like them!'

He snorted, then shook himself like a dog, a symbolical shedding of his rage.

'What did you want to check with me, Bob?'

'About these signals. Any ideas?'

'I have one.' Felix thrust himself into the conversation. 'What about Abic?'

'Abic?' Bob looked blank, Jeff thoughtful.

'It could be,' he mused. 'Yes, it probably is. If those signals are emitted from a brain then that could be the answer. Big signals, big brain, and Abic is the biggest thing in cortexes known. It makes sense, Bob.'

'The obvious always does,' said Bob ruefully, 'when it's shoved in your face, that is. We'll have to check it out though.'

'I'd like to help on that.' Felix shrugged at their expressions. 'My work's finished outside and there's nothing I can do until my equipment arrives. I'd like to keep busy.'

'Sure . . . ' Bob broke off as he looked at the screen. 'Here she goes!'

It was always a fine sight, better in the airlessness of space when the clear, sharp flame of the rockets was undiffused by atmosphere. For a moment the rocket hung, the base wreathed in flame then, slowly at first but with rapidly mounting velocity, it rose from the moon. The cameras followed its flight.

'Happy landings,' breathed Bob.

'They'll make it in one piece,' grumbled Jeff. 'If it wasn't for the fact I like Captain Star I'd wish they would break their necks.'

The ship had vanished from sight now, only the eye-bright exhaust showing stark against the night of space. Suddenly the spot of light grew, expanding until it almost filled the screen with almost unbearable brilliance.

They all knew what it meant.

12

It had been an interesting period. Lying supine on his bed Felix mentally reviewed the events since the sudden disruption of the ship. First there had been an instant of stunned silence and then, even before the flare of the explosion had faded from the screen, the intercom had broken into strident life.

'Hear this! Hear this! Major Crombie speaking. Attention all personnel! The vessel bearing the members of the Royal Commission back to Earth has exploded with the total destruction of all on board. All personnel will immediately proceed to their quarters and there remain. I will repeat that. All personnel will immediately proceed to their quarters and there remain.'

The results had given Felix food for thought.

One of the things he had learned early in his career was the axiom constantly preached to all student anthropologists; to know a culture you must understand it. The eating of human flesh is not peculiar behaviour in a society which practices cannibalism. The same axiom was more than applicable to individuals, as any psychologist knew. First find the normal pattern of behaviour and then, but only then, look for aberrations.

Felix had been sent to the station to look for aberrations among the personnel as a whole.

Seldon had reported sensing something odd and that, among a group controlling such horrible power was something which reeked of potential danger.

Felix stared at the chiselled stone of the roof. He had assessed the station as a group which had slipped from its original purpose. Discipline had seemed non-existent, the social barriers had vanished and the expected order had dissolved into apparent anarchy. It was reasonable to assume that, in any real emergency, such a group would react in a near-mob manner.

Instead they had acted with instinctive,

Guard-like discipline. There had been no talking, no argument, no speculation. There had been an intensive flurry of purposeful movement and that had been all.

It was another odd fact to add to the rest Felix had gathered and had created in his mind a question to which he still had to find the answer.

He turned as the door swung open, swinging from the bed as Echlan entered the room. The sergeant was apologetic.

'I'm sorry, Felix, but we have to search your quarters.'

'Major's orders?'

'Yes. Everyone has to go through it.'

Echlan jerked his head and two men entered from the corridor. They carried electronic equipment and began to run long electrodes up the sides of the room, standing one at each end. A thin, high humming sound came from a pack one carried on his back. Echlan saw Felix watching the operation.

'We're running a current through the rock,' he explained. 'If it isn't homogeneous the sound will alter from the detector. But you'd know all about that.'

Felix nodded, wondering if Echlan was using standard equipment or something which Howard had built for the purpose. Standard, he guessed, from the smoothly machined finish but the electronic engineer may well have improved the original model.

The room electronically swept, the men concentrated on the furnishings. Finally the man with the detector pack shook his head.

'Nothing so far, Sarge.'

'Right,' said Echlan. 'Stand over here, Felix, this won't take long. Right, Sam.'

Sam lowered a faceplate and, his companion standing behind Felix, carefully scanned every inch of his body.

'Something here,' he grunted hollowly. 'Metal. Fillings by the look of it.'

'Solid?'

Felix felt a sudden tingle in his mouth and tasted salt. He swore as violent agony stabbed from several molars.

'Sorry.' Sam lifted his faceplate. 'Those eddy-currents can play hell but its the only way to be sure.' He glanced at the sergeant. 'He's clear.'

'Good. Take the next in line.' Sombrely Echland watched his men file past then shook his head at Felix. 'This,' he said with feeling, 'is a hell of a job.'

'Do you think you'll find anything?'

'No, but we've got to be certain. Something blew up that rocket.'

'It could have been an accident. A component failure, for example.'

'Sure, and it probably was, but we've got to go through the routine.' Echlan looked tired and Felix guessed that he had been working at top pressure since the explosion. He hesitated as he turned towards the door. 'Hell, I almost forgot. Bob said you wanted to check over these.' He produced a wad of papers from a pocket. 'Some are from him the others are from Jeff. He said you'd know all about them.'

They would be the records from the encephalograph and Rasch's detector. Felix took them from the sergeant's hand.

'Thank you, I've been expecting them. When will the restriction be over?'

'You'll be informed.' Echlan looked

back from the corridor. 'You can go down the corridor to the toilet but no further. Don't try to leave this area, Felix. I've posted guards with orders to shoot if anyone tries to break out.' He managed a smile. 'Well, have fun.'

He left and Felix could sympathise with him. Searching the entire station, even with the most modern of equipment, was no easy job. And, he thought grimly, even if they found nothing there would always remain a doubt. If the ship had been sabotaged it would have destroyed all evidence along with itself.

★　★　★

He sighed and turned to the papers.

Felix was no stranger to encephalograms. Too often he had studied the erratic lines which signalled the presence of a cerebral tumour or the subtle variations which warned of abnormality. These records were not from a human cortex but the ones from Abic bore certain disturbing similarities . . . disturbing because Abic was artificial and, if man could make a facsimile of a human brain, then what did that make man?'

He shrugged, dismissing the concept. Like Ottoway he had no patience with theological speculation. In his experience mankind held within itself the attributes of both God and the Devil with the latter, at the present time well in the ascendency.

The graphs from Rasch's detector were interesting but told him little. At irregular intervals the stylo had traced peaks of varying height from the base line so that the record looked, when unrolled, like a two-dimensional profile map of a distant mountain range. He frowned at the graphs, noting one extremely high peak towards the end of the record.

If the variable line represented a message such a peak would signify a burst of extremely powerful transmission but Howard had sworn, and Felix was inclined to agree, that the graph had not recorded a message.

He picked up the encephalogram from the artificial brain. On this the red, alpha line was the erratic factor and he studied it, absently moving the two rolls so that the time-stamped edges corresponded. The high peak towards the end of Rasch's detector record coincided with another at almost the same time on Abic's graph. It wasn't one hundred per cent proof but it was so obvious that the academical doubt could be ignored.

Rasch's device had recorded the emissions from the artificial brain.

They had not been secret messages from a spy.

It had been a false alarm but the Americans could hardly be blamed for that. They hadn't known of the thing in the box and had been rightly suspicious of the mysterious signals. If their visit hadn't ended in tragedy the whole thing would have been amusing. Even so Rasch had built better than he knew. His record followed the encephalogram with startling accuracy.

Something clicked in Felix's brain. For a long moment he stared at the coupled graphs then rose and went to the intercom.

'Control.'

'Felix Larsen. Will you please tell me the exact time the rocket exploded.'

'One moment.'

He waited, finger hard on the button, guessing that the woman was checking on his request. Then her voice echoed softly from the speaker.

'The exact time was ten, eighteen, thirty-five.'

'Thank you.'

The timing was a little out, not much, but a shade early. Rasch's detector read 10.18.28, but Bob could have been a little careless in his setting or the drum may not have been synchronised with the station chronometer. Abic's time was far more accurate; only two seconds early and that time was exact. Allowing for the time-lag between the actual explosion and the visible evidence of the destruction received by control Abic had registered exactly as the rocket had exploded.

★   ★   ★

Major Crombie looked even more fatigued than Echlan but he was an older man and

165

carried a heavier weight of responsibility. He strode into the room, slammed the thick folder he carried down on the table and glared at Felix.

'Well?'

'I've found something I think you should see, Major.'

'So you said on the intercom. Has it anything to do with your wanting to know the exact time the rocket exploded?'

'Yes.' Felix smiled. 'You would know about that, of course. To be frank I hardly expected an answer to my request.'

'Why not? There's nothing secret about it.' Crombie sat on the bed, his shoulders slumped a little from their normal, ramrod rigidity. 'What is it I should know?'

Felix told him, pointing out the marks on both graphs but concentrating on the one from the artificial brain. Crombie nodded, his eyes shrewd.

'It could be coincidence,' he suggested.

'It could,' agreed Felix. 'It could also be a reverse-signal, Abic registered to the explosion of the rocket instead of the rocket exploding in exact time to a signal from Abic, but I doubt it.'

'It seems a logical explanation to me.'

Crombie, Felix thought, was either being very stupid or very cunning, and he knew the Major was far from being stupid. He took a deep breath. If the Major wanted him to bring it right out into the open then he would oblige.

'I could also,' he said carefully, 'be the work of a saboteur.'

Crombie raised his eyebrows.

'Abic could either be, or its housing could contain, some instrument which could be used for something other than what it appears.' Felix pointed to the graphs. 'Suppose, for example, that some mechanism had been planted in the rocket, a radio-controlled trigger, perhaps, or something like that. On receiving a special signal . . . ' He made an expressive gesture. 'It's possible, you know.'

'Agreed, but you overlook one point.' Crombie reached for his folder. 'Someone would have to plant the mechanism and send the signal. Now we aren't quite stupid here and neither are we as careless as you seem to think. No one worked on the rocket without supervision. Captain Star personally checked his vessel and none of our technicians went aboard unless accompanied by a member of the crew. It is just possible, I suppose, that one of them would be willing to sacrifice his life to destroy the vessel but it isn't likely. In any event, if that were so, he wouldn't need other assistance.'

Felix nodded.

'Now, as to sending a signal via Abic.' Crombie rifled the sheets of his folder. 'I have here a full account of everyone's movements for some time prior to the explosion. You were with Bob Howard and Jeff Carter in the electronics laboratory. Right?'

'That's correct.'

'Only Jeff and Reginald Ottoway have access to the bio-physical laboratory where Abic is installed. Jeff was with you and Reg was with Gloria in the hospital. The laboratory was deserted.'

'Couldn't someone have sneaked in?'

'No. The place is guarded and, unless either Ottoway or Carter is there, no one is allowed in.' He anticipated Felix's next question. 'The guard was on duty at all times, there's no mistake about that. He couldn't have sneaked in either.'

It seemed conclusive proof but Felix wasn't satisfied. He had sensed Ottoway's smouldering rage and he knew how highly Jeff regarded all politicians. Hate and detestation were a long way from murder but a man who hated deeply enough would not regard the destruction of the thing he hated as murder at all. To him it would be a justifiable elimination for the common good. He had met such personalities before.

Felix shook his head. He was being more than unfair, he was being ridiculously stupid. If Crombie had eliminated both Jeff and Reginald from suspicion then it was idiotic of him to insist on their guilt. But there was one last probability.

'There could have been a time-switch,' he pointed out. 'This is wild speculation, I admit, but it is a faint possibility.'

'True.' Crombie wasn't annoyed. He must, Felix realised, have become accustomed to searching out and eliminating every trace and shadow of possibility. 'That is why, as a standard precautionary measure, the departure of the rocket was delayed while I made a last-minute check-up.'

'I'm sorry.' Felix was sincere. Crombie shrugged.

'What for? You had both a right and a duty to report your suspicions to me as you did. You had an equal right and duty to remind me of what you thought I may have overlooked.' He rose and picked up his folder. The slump of his shoulders was very noticeable and, as if conscious of it, he made an effort to straighten.

'A bad business this,' he said. 'A damn bad business. I don't know what's going to become of it.'

'It was an accident.'

'I know, but some accidents shouldn't happen. This was one of them.'

It was the finish of his ambition and Crombie must know it. One way or another he had reached the end of his career. Felix remembered something as the Major reached the door.

'What about Leaver?'

'Leaver?' Crombie halted and turned, a frown creasing his forehead.

'Yes.' Felix was carefully casual. Seldon had told him of the man but, as yet, he hadn't been able to locate him. If, as Seldon had hinted, the man was suspect then Crombie should know. 'I've heard his name mentioned,' he explained. 'Just casual gossip, you know. But I can't remember seeing him around.'

'I'm not surprised.'

'Do you know him?'

'I did.' Crombie was grim. 'He's dead.'

'Dead!'

'Yes, some time ago now. I suppose you heard Avril talk about him but it's a wonder she didn't tell you. He was her . . . ' Crombie coughed. ' . . . well, you know.'

It was odd how, even in this free and easy society, the old delicacy still persisted.

13

A deep voice was singing an improvised song.

'That's nice.' Avril smelt of roses, probably some concoction brewed in one of the laboratories. Women, no matter where they were, would always find means of adornment. 'I like to hear people singing, do you?'

'Sometimes.'

'Only sometimes? Don't you like it?'

'Not very much.' Felix didn't like calypso even when well constructed and well sung and this was neither.

'Sad sack!' She shook his arm. 'Something on your mind, pet?'

'No.'

'Are you sure? You look as if you've got the cares of the world on your shoulders. Would you like me to take your mind off them for you?'

'Please! I tell you there's nothing wrong.'

'Yes there is.' She halted, facing him in the narrow passage, her face serious. 'You've been down in the mouth ever since the restriction's been lifted. Are you still brooding over that rocket?'

'No.'

'Then what's the matter? I thought you'd like me to call for you. I got tired of waiting for you to call for me. Now I wish that I hadn't.' She squeezed his arm. 'Please tell me, Felix.'

'Does something always have to be wrong because I'm not grinning like a Cheshire Cat?' He saw that he was hurting her and took a perverse delight in his power. 'If you don't like my company then why do you keep chasing me?'

'I . . . ' She bit her lip. 'I'm sorry. It's just that . . . '

'Well?'

'Do I chase you?'

'Yes.'

'I see.' She dropped his arm. 'It won't happen again. I've been a fool, I suppose, but did you have to make me feel so cheap?'

Stubbornly he remained silent, trying

not to see how pathetic she looked, how much like an unwanted kitten. The yearning to take her in his arms was almost irresistible.

'Goodbye, Felix.' She managed a smile. 'There's no need for us to part bad friends. We can't help seeing each other sometimes but I'll try not to be a nuisance.' Then her armour cracked a little. 'Damn you! Why did you have to come to the Moon? Why did I have to fall in love with you?'

'As you did with Leaver?'

He saw the shock on her face and then the sudden dawn of understanding.

'Leaver is dead, Felix.'

'So I've been told. But you loved him.'

'Yes. I loved him.'

There was no shame in her eyes and, he realised, no cause for shame. There was no regret either and for the same reason. Whatever had been between them was over but his mind couldn't accept that. He was suffering from jealousy and felt a sick self-contempt because of it. He was a mature, experienced adult not a pimply-faced schoolboy or a gangling adolescent. Jealousy was foreign to his nature and had no part either of his character or training.

But he was jealous and he knew why.

And so did she.

'I loved him,' she repeated. 'But that was a long time ago and it's all over now. I'm not mourning his memory if that's what you think. And I'm not looking for a substitute. Not now. Not since I met you.'

'Avril! I . . . '

'You're jealous, Felix. I should take it as a compliment. Would you take it that way if I were jealous of your ex-wife?'

'That would be unreasonable.'

'Yes.' Her eyes were very direct. 'It would, wouldn't it?'

She turned and left him, walking very straight, looking very slim but she was no longer sad and it was no longer goodbye. Felix loved her and she knew it. One day he would admit it. She could afford to wait.

★　★　★

Howard wasn't in his laboratory. His assistant, a mouse-coloured man with the improbable name of Tan Bark, looked up from where he sat at a drawing board as Felix entered.

'You looking for Bob?'

'I've just brought back some papers he loaned me.'

'The Rasch detector graphs?' Bark gestured towards the apparatus. 'Dump them down if you've finished with them. Did you get anything interesting?'

'Not more than we expected. Rasch's apparatus registers the emission from Abic.'

'It's a wonder it does anything at all,' snorted Bark. 'It reminds me of the junk I used to throw together when I was a kid before I learned how not to do things. I'm surprised at the Yanks wasting their time on such rubbish.'

'Naturally,' said Felix drily. 'Where is Bob, anyway?'

'Working on this baby.' Bark rapped a knuckle on his drawing board. Felix leaned over his shoulder to look at the plans. He frowned at what he saw.

'You've seen this in a laboratory,' said Bark with undisguised enthusiasm. 'It's one of those things we knock up to please the visitors and it makes a handy demonstration of magnetism. Out here it could be useful too.'

It could, thought Felix grimly, be more than useful. Magnetic acceleration wasn't new but on Earth it had its limitations. Basically it was a series of hollow electromagnets which could be activated in turn thus dragging any ferrous mass through their coils along a linear path. The more magnets the greater the speed with acceleration mounting in geometrical progression. Bark's plan showed a truly gigantic installation with dozens of electro-magnets.

'What's the idea?'

'Nothing serious, though I suppose it could be useful.' Bark leaned back, his face thoughtful. 'We could fire a mass of small ball-bearings along it with a jerking mechanism at the far end to send them out in a spray like a shotgun blast. With the speed they would travel, an attacking ship would be riddled like a sieve.'

'If it was coming along the right path,' reminded Felix. Bark shrugged.

'Sure, but that's no real objection. Any attacking ship would have to line up with the station approach and this thing could be set to really spread the missiles. The range would be out of this world, remember. Escape velocity's only over a mile a second and we could reach that without trouble.' He grinned at Felix. 'You should talk to Bob about it. It could make your lasers look sick.'

'I doubt it. You haven't manoeuvrability for one thing and there's a time lag for another. Still, I will talk to him later.' Felix hesitated. 'Have you built it yet?'

'Not yet. Maybe we won't ever but it's fun getting it ready just in case. Mental recreation, you know, we've got to stay sane and healthy.'

'Of course.'

'Shall I page Bob for you?'

'No. I've got to see Jeff. Tell Bob I delivered the graphs.'

'Sure. Have fun.'

Fun could have peculiar annotations. Digging caverns in the rock for recreation was amusing as well as beneficial. Building electro-magnetic acceleration devices was both mentally stimulating and provided a means of keeping skills in condition. Add them both and the result could be far from amusing.

Especially when it was remembered just what the station produced.

Felix doubted if the Government would approve. He doubted if any sane and reasonable man would sleep well at night if he knew that above his head hung a damoclean sword.

A sword composed of carefully dug chambers which could be used as missile-proof feeding magazines. A gigantic magnetic-accelerator powered with the energy of an atomic pile and which could easily fling small metal canisters into space at well over Luna escape velocity.

Canisters which could not help but fall on the Earth and which could be filled with the minute horrors bred in the laboratories of the station.

14

Jeff was busy when Felix arrived in the bio-physical laboratory. He looked up from the artificial brain, a testing instrument in his hand.

'Anything wrong?'

'No, just a routine testing.' Jeff straightened and attached his instrument to a different part of the structure. 'Did you check out the graphs?'

'Yes. It was as we suspected.'

'No spy, uh?'

'Not unless Abic's the traitor.'

'Come again?'

'It sent out a signal coinciding with the explosion.'

'I see.' Jeff carefully finished his testing then ducked from within the barrier. He rested his instrument on a bench, made a notation on a pad then grunted with satisfaction. 'That should hold him for a while.'

'Him?'

'Why not? We've given him a body of sorts, a name of a kind and a mission in life. Why deny him a name?'

'No reason, but why not her?'

'With a name like Abic?' Jeff frowned. 'Still, why not? I knew a girl named Abbie once, and then there's weirder names than that. Still, to me he's masculine all the way through.' He leaned against the barrier. 'So he sent out a signal, did he? Maybe he was waving them goodbye.'

'If he did it was a permanent farewell.' Felix was puzzled. 'You're not taking this seriously, are you?'

'You're mistaken. I'm deadly serious about everything and anything to do with Abic. But there is such a thing as coincidence, you know.'

'Admitted.'

'And he could have registered the explosion rather than vice-versa.'

'True, if the timing had been different, but the signal was early, not late.'

'That proves nothing. We could have seen the results of the explosion seconds after it actually happened,' pointed out Jeff. 'And we don't know what, if anything, Abic registered. Maybe he recorded a fear-impression from one of the crew.'

'Is that possible?'

Jeff smiled and Felix grew thoughtful. It seemed a ridiculous concept and yet, if Rasch could build a thing of metal, crystal and wire which could register the emissions of a brain, then why should not a brain be able to register the strong emotions of another?

'You intrigue me, Jeff,' he said. 'I'd like to work on it. Have you any earlier encephalograms?'

'As many as you want from the day we fixed the connections.' Jeff gestured to a tall filing cabinet. 'Help yourself.'

'I will.' Felix frowned at the stacked sheets on which the graphs had been transferred. 'I'll take those of the past few months if I may. Where do I begin?'

'I'll get them for you.'

Felix stepped back as Jeff riffled through the sheets, sensing, for some reason, a hint of aggression in the other's manner. He wondered if it could be a touch of professional jealousy, the dislike of an outsider taking an interest in what could be regarded as personal property. It was probably a mistaken impression, the result of his own hypertense nerves, and he knew it was dangerous when weighing others to trust instinct too far.

He sighed and leaned on the rail, staring at the enigmatic box which housed the largest brain known to man. A bank of dials recorded essential information and, as a supposed electronic expert, he should have been able to read them like a book. But he was a psychologist, not an electrician, and the box held nothing from which he could gain information. No eyes, ears, mouth. No tiny muscles to tense under strain and signal change of emotion. No hands which so often told more than they knew. No tongue which spoke truth when its owner intended lies. No glands to secrete odours which were the signals of the primitive nature guiding all basic motivations.

Nothing but some erratic lines scratched by pens on a roll of marked paper.

He turned as Jeff came from the

cabinet, papers piled high in his hands.

'Here, Felix, these should keep you busy for a long time to come. Are you interested in cyphers?'

'A little. Why?'

'Because these are a cypher.' Jeff handed them over. 'Personally I can't see how you could possibly make anything of them but you're welcome to try.'

'Thanks,' said Felix drily. 'It's good of you to let me amuse myself.'

He glanced at the sheets noting that the graphs had been cut and stuck on pasteboard for easy handling. Idly he riffled the stack glancing at the dates stamped along the upper edge of each graph. Each sheet held twelve hours and he tensed as a date caught his eye. It was one he would never forget.

'Seen anything?' Jeff was at his elbow.

'Nothing important.' Felix tucked the sheets under his arm. 'Well, I'll let you get back to work.'

He had lied but that wasn't important. He had only done it because of the other's aggressiveness. What was important was that he had seen something which had caused a surge of adrenalin to quicken his blood. A date and a time. *Dec. 13th. 22.5.23.*

The time of his accident!

Beneath it soared a thin red line.

* * *

Avril was puzzled. 'But why do you want it, Felix? What interest can the hospital register have for you?'

'I want to check up on something. I've tried to get it myself but the guard won't let me through.'

'Naturally, not without permission from Gloria.'

'But you can get in without any argument. You've a right, as dietician, to enter the hospital at any time. Please, Avril, I wouldn't ask if it wasn't important.'

He was taking a chance but it was a calculated risk. Of all the station personnel she was the one who would be most likely to help him without question. She loved him and, to her, that should be reason enough. But still she hesitated.

'I don't understand this. Why can't you just ask Gloria to let you look at it?'

'Because I'm not sure and I don't want to make myself look a fool.' He smiled, hoping that she wouldn't continue the line of questioning. 'It's just something I want to check out, Avril. I'm probably all wrong but, if I'm not, then I'll tell Gloria all about it. If I bother her with it now she might get all sorts of wrong ideas about me. You know how she is with her pills and probing.'

'But — '

'Please, Avril. Couldn't you do it just for me?'

Put like that he knew she couldn't refuse.

Later, with the book in his hands, he wondered why he had acted so mysteriously. Caution bred caution until it defeated its own end. He had given reason for Avril to wonder about him and that could be the first crack in the armour of his disguise. Worse, she may begin to get suspicious of his loyalty and, if that happened, he would have to reveal himself.

He wondered if Leaver had used her in the same way.

Irritably he concentrated on the register trying to forget the dead man.

The book, like Gloria, was neat, the handwriting small and well formed, each entry clear and unambiguous. With the heap of graphs at his side Felix quickly correlated the dates then checked the high peaks with the entries in the book.

They matched.

There was a slight difference in the times but that could be explained by careless recording on the part of the doctor. She would not have been concerned with seconds and only with the actual time of admission. His own entry was minutes later than Abic's record; but it had taken time for him to fall, more time for him to be rescued. The other entries could be explained in the same way.

It was not coincidence. It could not have been coincidence, the records matched too well for that. There had to be another explanation.

Felix remembered what Jeff had suggested. Abic could be registering simple human emotion and, if it was, then it must be registering the emotion of fear. But if that were so how to account for Maynard's suicide attempt? A man determined to kill himself does not feel fear. Hate, perhaps, depression but not fear. Fear would defeat his own object. Fear was the emotion which kept criminals alive when all they had to face was execution. They were more afraid of immediate death than later destruction.

But if not fear then what?'

Grimly Felix leafed through the register, concentrating this time on the actual entries and not just on their times. Most were due to accidents, natural in an establishment like the station, and it was these he found most intriguing.

Two women had tried to commit suicide at various times by hanging themselves from nylon rope tested to one thousand pounds earth weight. Each time the 'unbreakable' rope had snapped.

A man had deliberately gripped a pair of heavy duty electric cables — and had been thrown clear with minor searing on the skin.

A technician had deliberately slashed his wrists. He had then stumbled against a bench, knocked over a container of liquid plastic which had sealed his wounds, and had suffered only mild shock.

Carl Leaver had fallen a distance of ten feet and had broken his neck.

Ten feet! On Earth that would be equivalent to a fall of eighteen inches. Felix wondered if Seldon had known what had happened to his suspected spy, then turned up the man's own entry.

. . . *Seldon. Caught in fall of rock from roof.*

Extensive amputations.

Sickly Felix wondered just how extensive those amputations had been.

The guard was sympathetic.

'Is it bad, Felix?'

'I hope not.' Felix managed to give the impression that he felt a lot worse than he looked. 'It's just that I'm getting dizzy spells and I want to let Gloria check me over in case there's anything wrong. Did she notify you I was coming?'

'Sure.' The guard jerked his head

towards the door of the hospital. 'You'd better wait inside.'

'Is Gloria there?' Felix knew she wasn't.

'No, but you can go inside.'

The place was as he remembered it. The same neat, empty ward, the tidy office with its filed records. Pulling the register from beneath his coverall he placed it on the desk where it had been before. There had been no need to implicate Avril any further and he wanted to see Seldon.

The door of the operating theatre was locked.

Irritably he tested the catch, wondering why Gloria had locked it at all, then forgetting his wonder in a mounting sense of urgency. Frowning he examined the simple mechanism then crossed to a cabinet of surgical instruments. One was shaped like a long, thin, slightly curved spatula, probably something with which to hold down a tongue, but it would serve a different purpose. He probed, strained, probed again and the lock clicked open.

Seldon was asleep.

He was in the same position, the same sheet pulled tight around his throat, still in the odd, humped posture which hinted of terrible injuries. His eyes were closed and the lines of his face sagged in relaxation. He looked, thought Felix, very old and very tired.

'Seldon!'

No response.

'Seldon, damn you! Wake up!'

He couldn't shout, the guard was outside and he couldn't rely on the acoustics of the place. Even a whisper might be overheard. Reaching out he squeezed the man's cheeks.

'Seldon!'

The skin was flaccid beneath his fingers, cold and somehow reptilian as if the life within flowed with alien sluggishness. The theatre was very quiet, only a thin susurration came from beneath Seldon's sheet as if a tiny pump were working with smooth efficiency.

'Seldon!'

Felix had to talk to him, there were questions to which he must have answers, but still the man remained asleep. Losing patience Felix clamped his hand over the man's nostrils and mouth.

It would have woken any normal man. The threat of suffocation would have dragged any breathing creature from the deepest sleep but still Seldon did not waken. Standing there, his hand tight over the other's mouth, Felix felt the hairs prickle on the base of his neck and something cold traced a path down his spine.

There was one way to be certain.

The spatula was of polished alloy, light but strong and reflecting the light in shining sterility. Removing his hand he held it before Seldon's mouth, watching for the tell-tale misting which would signify life.

He was still watching when Gloria entered the room.

15

There had been no warning, not even the sound of the outer door opening, but perhaps he hadn't been intended to hear. He straightened, the spatula still gleaming unmisted in his hand and he looked down at it, placing it carefully on a small table before looking at the doctor.

She wasn't alone. Avril was beside her and, behind them both, Crombie stood grim and alert. He held his pistol and Felix wondered if he would use it. Then he saw the Major's expression and knew that he wouldn't hesitate to shoot.

'Felix!' Avril stepped forward. 'I . . . '

'You told them.' He felt bitter at her betrayal.

'She told us nothing,' snapped Crombie. He took hold of Avril's arm and pulled her to his side away from the line of fire. 'She didn't have to. You've been under surveillance from the moment you arrived.'

'Normal procedure surely, Major?'

'Yes. You tried to flatter me on the subject once before, I suppose you thought that you were being clever. But you aren't clever, Larsen. Your biggest mistake was in enquiring after Leaver. There was no way you could have known about him had you been what you claimed to be.'

'Do you honestly believe that I'm an enemy agent?' The concept was so ridiculous that Felix fought the desire to laugh. He lost the impulse as he looked at Crombie's eyes. The man was serious and Felix couldn't blame him. He had only himself to blame for his position.

'You're not an electronics engineer,' said Crombie. 'Bob Howard spotted that almost right away.'

'How?'

'You didn't talk his language. The details are unimportant but he guessed there was something wrong.'

'I see. Have you considered that Bob might have his own reasons for making me a scapegoat?'

'That is a cheap accusation,' said

Crombie. 'But I've investigated all possibilities. You asked after Leaver and you persuaded Avril to take the register from the hospital. Neither is the act of an innocent man.'

'It needn't be the act of an enemy agent either,' reminded Felix. 'As it happens I have a perfectly innocent explanation for both. So you knew about Leaver?'

'I suspected him. He died before that suspicion became proof.'

'You weren't the only one, Major. Seldon suspected him too. He told me about him when I was here after my accident. That was why I mentioned him to you. I thought you should know.'

'Interesting.' Crombie snapped up his pistol as Felix stepped away from where he stood. 'Don't try anything Larsen! There is a lot you can tell us so I want to keep you alive. But I'm a good shot and I won't have to kill you if you're thinking of trying anything stupid.'

'Don't be ridiculous!' Felix snorted his impatience. 'Just because you've found out something you can't explain you assume that I'm an enemy. Well, I'm not.

Seldon told me about Leaver. If he wasn't dead he could prove what I say.'

'Dead!' Gloria surged forward forgetful of being in line with Crombie's gun. He moved quickly to one side.

'Careful, Larsen!'

'Don't be a fool!' Felix turned to the doctor. 'I'm sorry, I should have told you earlier. I was trying to determine if he was alive when you came in. There's no sign of breathing.'

'No,' she said calmly. 'There wouldn't be. But Seldon isn't dead.'

Felix raised his eyebrows. In his experience when a man didn't breathe then that man was dead. He watched as Gloria moved the sheet from around Seldon's throat revealing a cabinet studded with dials and controls. She adjusted a dial, waited a few moments then threw a small switch. The soft susurration Felix had heard earlier rose to a thin hum.

Seldon opened his eyes.

★　★　★

His name should have been Lazarus. Felix would have sworn that he was dead, every test he had been able to administer had proved that, but now he was alive, his eyes wide open, the lips working with a soft smacking sound.

'Hello, Gloria. I see we've got company.' He frowned as he looked at Felix, his eyes rolling in their sockets. 'Haven't I seen you somewhere before?'

'Yes.' Felix stepped before the cabinet. 'I spoke with you, remember? We talked and . . .'

'That's enough, Larsen!' Crombie shouldered him to one side. 'Listen, Seldon, this is very important. Did you talk about anyone to this man?'

'Who?'

'That's what I want you to tell me. Think now, did you?'

'We talked of all kinds of things.' Seldon paused, the tip of his tongue touching his lips. 'Could I have a drink, please?'

'Later. Well?'

'I may have mentioned Leaver. Yes, I did mention Leaver now I come to think

197

of it. Please! Could I have that drink now?'

'I'll get it.' Felix crossed to the faucet and filled the spouted cup. Carefully he held it to Seldon's lips, letting a trickle of moisture moisten his mouth. He straightened, conscious of Gloria's eyes watching his every move.

'You've done that before,' she said. He shrugged.

'I told you that I'd talked with Seldon.' He set aside the cup. 'Now, there's one thing I must know. When you had your accident, Seldon, what was in . . . '

'No!' Gloria pushed him aside with unsuspected strength. 'You are not to talk about that.'

'But — '

'No!'

Quickly she adjusted a control and the soft pulse of the pump faded to a murmuring whisper. Seldon's eyelids drooped and, even as Felix watched, he regained his former immobility.

'You've read the register,' said Gloria softly. 'The amputations were . . . extreme. The rock fall crushed the pelvis, ruptured the spleen and shredded the lungs with broken fragments of ribs. Fortunately the biophysical laboratory had a second artificial blood pump and I managed to connect the great arteries of the cortex with the supply. Even so it was a near thing. I managed to save the larynx, most of his spine and the upper trachea but the rest . . . ' She made an expressive gesture.

'Amputated!'

Felix felt a little sick. Seldon was now nothing more than a head connected to an artificial blood supply and a pump to force air through his throat so that he could speak. It was, he had no doubt, a miracle of modern surgery, perhaps possible only on the moon, but his instinctive humanity revolted at the concept of such a helpless cripple. Gloria must have read his thoughts.

'You are disgusted,' she said, 'but that is your conservatism, not your logic. Seldon is alive and will remain so indefinitely, subject, of course, to the normal catabolic decay of the flesh of his face and skull. Even so that may be delayed long past the normal life-expectancy.'

'You call it life?'

'He is aware. He can see and hear and speak. Also, he can hope.'

'For a new body, I suppose?' Felix was bitter. 'Why don't you just kill him and have done with it?'

'That would be murder.'

'Of course. You mustn't do that. You doctors are all alike. It doesn't matter what human suffering you inflict, it's all right because you're within the law. Damn it! You wouldn't let a dog suffer like that. No, I'm wrong. You do let dogs suffer even worse. Are you a disciple of Pavlov, Doctor Brittain?'

'That's enough, Larsen!'

'Is it, Major? Am I insulting the good doctor?' Felix gritted his teeth. 'Well, perhaps I am, but why can't I speak to Seldon if he's so happy?'

'I didn't claim that he was happy,' said Gloria evenly. 'How could any man in his position be that? But I don't want to inflict further mental agony. The psychic shock of the accident was tremendous and he still hasn't got over it. That is why we keep him under minimum wakefulness. Hypnosis has helped a great deal, sometimes he doesn't even know that he has no body, but outside disturbances could send him into catatonia.'

'Would that be so bad? He wouldn't be the first to find escape into the past.'

'Now you are talking utter nonsense and you know it. There is not, nor can there ever be, escape into the past. Always there are troubles and the mind retreats and retreats until it is back in the foetal stage and can retreat no further. Seldon has a fine mind. I intend to save it from that.'

'So that he can live a head on a box?'

'Is it so much worse than living in an iron lung? Be reasonable, Felix. We are working all the time on new prosthetic devices but before we can even try to fit them, his body and mind must heal.'

'All right.' Felix drew a deep breath. 'Let's forget the argument. I'll accept that your motives are good. In fact I'll apologise for doubting them. I'm sorry, Gloria. I mean that.' He stared at Crombie. 'Well, are you satisfied?'

'Of your innocence? No.'

'But you heard Seldon say that he had told me about Leaver.'

'I did.'

'Then what other proof do you need?'

'Let's get one thing straight,' said Crombie. 'Since the rocket exploded this station has been in a state of emergency. Even without that I am in complete charge as regards any suspected activities. I do not need proof. I do not even require suspicion. Doubt is sufficient. You are not free of doubt.'

'But — '

'There are no buts. The security of the station is of paramount importance.'

It was time to take control of the situation. Felix looked around the operating theatre then stepped towards the door. He heard the sharp intake of Avril's breath and sensed rather than saw the movement of Crombie's gun. He turned and looked directly at the Major.

'If you're going to shoot, Major, do it now. If not I suggest we continue this discussion in more congenial surroundings.'

Meekly they followed him into the empty ward.

★   ★   ★

'Why,' said Gloria suddenly, 'did you want to speak to Seldon? What is so important that you are willing to risk his sanity to discover?'

She had been standing very silent, her eyes thoughtful as Crombie had made his accusations and Felix was reminded of a detached scientist studying a specimen. So he had often stood and watched, waiting for the moment of maximum psychological impact before asking the question which so often drove to the root of lies and truth. It was a technique used often by the police and he could admire it even though he was the subject of interrogation.

'I wanted to ask him about his accident.'

'Why?'

Felix hesitated. To be truthful was to expose himself and to make an end of his usefulness to the Government. Not that he could be of much further use but, if he had gauged the situation correctly, there was a very real danger that he would never be permitted to return to Earth. Yet he had to answer the question.

'I wanted to know all about it,' he said slowly. 'I wanted to know if the accident was just that or something else.'

'Deliberate sabotage?' Gloria glanced at the Major. 'How would Seldon know that?'

'He could sense it.' Felix tried to explain. 'He could have received an impression of wrongness. For example, his fellow workers could all, for no apparent reason, have left the workings at the same time. He could have been given a message which sent him there. I can't say what his impression could be but he may have had one.'

'He didn't.' Crombie looked at the pistol in his hand then thrust it into its holster. The gesture was symbolic and Felix felt the immediate easing of tension. 'I checked all that. It was a genuine accident.'

'Was he working alone?'

'No.'

'Yet he was the only one to be hurt. Didn't that strike you as rather odd? One man hurt, almost killed, in a rock fall and yet no one else even slightly injured. I've worked on those rock faces and there isn't a great deal of room.'

'Agreed, but it happened,' said Crombie drily. 'After all, accidents are usually odd. That's why they are accidents.'

'Yes,' said Felix deliberately. 'If they are normal accidents.'

'Sabotage? But I told you I checked every possibility. There was no sabotage.'

'I think I know what Felix is getting at,' said Gloria. She looked at him. 'Accident prones?'

'What,' said Avril, 'is an accident prone?'

'It is a person around which accidents seem to constantly happen,' said Gloria. 'They do not cause the accidents, quite often they are not personally involved, but wherever they happen to be there are accidents. Insurance companies know them quite well, in fact they have a black-list of such people, and they are the first thing any establishment like this has to weed out.'

'Have you weeded them out?'

'Yes, Felix. I've checked every accident with that in mind. There are no common personnel involved.'

'I'm not thinking of personnel,' said Felix. 'But you are wrong when you say there is no common factor involved.'

He told them what he had discovered. Gloria was thoughtful, Crombie frankly sceptical. Avril said nothing but, standing beside Felix, she softly squeezed his arm. He had, at least, one ally.

'We've been over all this,' snapped Crombie testily. 'Abic is obviously registering an emotional emission from those concerned.'

'That is what Jeff says but you could both be wrong. Look at it from the other direction. Abic emits something, a mental force, perhaps, certainly it is akin to thought or Rasch's detector wouldn't have registered it. It seems an odd coincidence that those emissions always coincide with an accident of some kind. And they do! I've proved it!'

'No.' Gloria was the cold scientist seeking faults in a seemingly perfect theory. 'You haven't you know, Felix. You have simply discovered a relationship but it need not mean what you say. The Major could be correct.'

'The Major is wrong!' Felix couldn't understand why they were so blind. 'Listen,' he said to Crombie. 'You've just told me that you don't need proof or suspicion. All you need is doubt. Well, for God's sake! Isn't there enough doubt here to satisfy you?'

'Be fair, Felix!' Gloria was still the scientist. 'You can't expect us to take your unsupported word when there is a perfectly rational explanation which, for some reason, you refuse to accept. If you had a shred of proof . . . '

'Proof! You want still more proof!'

Felix recognised his anger and forced himself to be calm. Shouting was no way to persuade these people.

'Very well,' he said evenly. 'You ask for proof and I can supply it. Avril! You will find some papers in my room. They are the encephalograms from Abic. You know what they look like?'

'Yes, Felix.'

'Will you get them for me. Hurry, please.' He looked grimly at the doctor as Avril left the room. 'Now, Gloria, for your proof. You must have the case history of Seldon in your files. Will you get it, please.'

'For what reason?'

'Please get it. I'll explain when Avril gets back.'

She wasn't long. By the flush on her face she had run both ways. Felix took the records and put them on one of the beds. Gloria sat beside them, her file in her lap.

'Now,' said Felix. 'I'll supply your proof. First I want you to check that the high points on the alpha line, that's the red line on the graphs, check with the accident times in the register. Will you get it for me, Avril.'

He waited as they made the check.

'Right? Good. Now if Abic is simply responding to the stimulus of some strong human emotion, pain or fear or terror, then it should do so each and every time. A detector does not choose when it is going to register. It is either operating or it is not and Abic is in continuous operation. Therefore, if Abic is the register-ing instrument you claim, there should be no gaps in its record.'

Felix riffled the graphs until he found the one he wanted.

'Open your file, please Gloria, the time of Seldon's accident was 21.54.49. Right?'

'Not exactly. I have it here as 21.56. I don't record the seconds.'

'I know, but it is near enough allowing for inevitable time lags. You see the alpha high point?'

He showed her the broken red line.

'Seldon, I take it, was unconscious when you found him and you probably gave him initial sedation and then followed with a course of extensive anaesthesia.'

'Naturally. I had to guard against shock.'

'Of course. But, inevitably, he had to waken. I assume that, when he did, he was horrified at discovering what had happened to him?'

'Well . . . '

'You told us that he was in actual danger of losing his sanity,' rapped Felix.

'You said that you had to use drugs and hypnosis to calm him. Is that correct?'

'It is.'

'Then he must have experienced strong emotion at that time. Pain and fear and terror. Is that so?'

'Yes.'

'Then those emotions must have registered on the encephalograms from Abic.'

Felix leaned forward and thrust the graphs into the doctor's hands.

'Please check, Gloria. You have the times Seldon woke in your file. You have admitted that he suffered strong emotions at those times. If abic is nothing but an emotion-detector then the alpha line should match your records.' Impatiently he waited as she frowned over the papers. 'Well, do they?'

He could read the answer in her face.

'They don't, do they?' He snatched the papers from her hands, checking times against the erratic red line. 'Nothing!' He flung down the records. 'It's as I thought. There's no correlation at all. Well, Major! There's your proof!'

16

Crombie surprised him.

'Gloria?'

If she made a signal Felix missed it but it didn't matter. She could not but help agree.

'I see.' Thoughtfully Crombie stared down at the scattered records. He did not pick them up to make his own check and Felix found that odd in a man who prided himself on fully investigating every possibility. His next words were even more strange.

'Just what,' he said carefully, 'do you think you have proven, Felix?'

'Isn't it obvious? Abic is emitting, not receiving.'

'So?'

'Are you serious, Major?' Felix had met scepticism before but nothing so blatant in a man he had previously considered so shrewd. 'Every time there is an accident that artificial brain sends out some mysterious force. Seldon's accident, my own, even the explosion of the rocket followed or coincided with peaks of that emission. Damn it! Can't you see that Abic didn't register those events — it caused them!'

'Please!' Crombie lifted one hand in an unmistakable gesture. He was a sensible adult talking to the foolish child. 'Let us keep a sense of proportion about this.'

'I don't understand you.' Felix felt his triumph at having proven his point dissolve into rage. He forced himself to be calm, taking deep breaths until he had regained his composure. 'Aren't you satisfied with the proof?'

Crombie shrugged. 'You have shown us that there is an oddity in the records and no doubt Ottoway will be very interested in what you have found but to state that Abic is responsible for several accidents and the destruction of the rocket . . . '

'Can there now be any doubt?'

'An artificial growth confined in a strong plastic box?' The Major smiled. 'Really, Felix! How can I be expected to believe that?'

'By using your intelligence,' rasped Felix. 'That is if you have any, which I'm beginning to doubt!'

'There is no need to be insulting!'

'You — '

Felix bit off the words as his anger mounted until it threatened his judgement. The fool! The stupid blind fool! And to think that such a man was in complete charge of station security!

Or was he the fool he appeared to be?

The anger resolved itself into a cold determination.

'Abic must be destroyed,' said Felix. 'The security of the station depends on it.'

'Don't be ridiculous!'

Crombie's gun was in its holster, the flap open, the polished butt reflecting the light in a warm, walnut sheen. Felix picked up some of the papers, let them fall and snatched at the gun as Crombie's attention was distracted.

'What — ' The Major clawed at his belt.

'Stay where you are!' Felix stepped back against the wall, the gun in his hand.

'Don't move and don't make a noise!'

'He means it, Major!' Gloria's even tones cut through Crombie's anger with a note of warning. He released his breath with a sigh.

'Felix!'

'Be quiet, Avril!' His eyes darted about the ward. 'That cabinet! There is a bottle of small blue pills in there. Bring them to me. Quickly now!'

He remembered the pills and he recognised the label. He smiled at Avril's strained face as she handed him the bottle.

'Felix! You can't . . . '

'I know what I'm doing.'

He gestured the woman back, smashed the bottle with a sweep of the gun and threw a shower of blue onto one of the beds.

'All right, Major. You first. Swallow three of those pills.'

'But — '

'They are very strong, Felix,' said Gloria quickly. He smiled without humour.

'I know just how strong they are, doctor. Well, Major? What are you waiting for?'

For a moment he thought that Crombie would refuse and his hand tightened on the gun, his finger pressing the trigger so that the hammer lifted from the breech. Then Gloria's voice ended the Major's hesitation.

'Do as he says, Jack!'

Slowly Crombie swallowed three of the pills.

'Good!' Felix relaxed his grip on the pistol. 'Now you, Gloria. That's right. Avril! Thank you.' He gestured with the gun. 'Now lie down. Just stretch out and relax. When you wake it will all be over.'

'You . . . ' Crombie made a supreme effort to resist the drug. He managed to heave himself up on one elbow and then, quite suddenly, fell back with a mumbling sigh.

Ten seconds later they were all unconscious.

There had been no choice.

Walking down the corridors, the sheaf of encephalograms shielding the bulk of the pistol under his coverall, Felix wasted no time on regret. He had assessed the situation, made his decision and was about to carry it out. Later, when the brain had been destroyed, he would reveal himself to the Director and claim protection from Sir Joseph. There would be questions, of course, and perhaps a board of inquiry, but it would be too late then to prevent essential action.

Nothing could stop that now.

Ottoway nodded a greeting from where he stood at a bench, a graduated flask of ruby liquid in his hand. Jeff was standing beside the cabinet holding the records.

'Busy?' Felix handed the graphs to Jeff.

'We're always busy.' Jeff scanned the records, grunted his pleasure at finding them in correct sequence and tucked them into the cabinet. 'Well, Felix, did you solve the cypher?'

'I think so.' Felix looked at Ottoway. 'Is that a Luna cocktail or have I interrupted an experiment?'

'Neither. I'm just checking Abic's blood. We want no bugs in this stuff we didn't put in ourselves.' He put down the flask. 'It seems O.K., Jeff.'

'Good.'

'What would you do if it wasn't?' Felix

leaned idly against the protective rail, moving so that both men were in the field of his vision.

'Do?' Ottoway shrugged. 'Drain and replenish, of course. We carry a spare stock in the deep freeze.'

'A complete exchange? Just like you would change the blood of a blue baby?'

'Yes.' Ottoway seemed surprised at the analogy. 'You could say that but it would be much simpler with Abic than with any baby. Anyway, we don't have to worry about that now.'

Not now nor ever, thought Felix grimly. Not now nor ever.

He glanced down at the thing he intended to destroy. The box housing the actual brain looked too strong and, while a bullet might penetrate, there was always the risk that it would do little damage if any. The instruments were obvious extensions and destroying them would do no real harm. The pump was another matter.

He stared at the plating covering the humped apparatus beneath the box. Within that covering would be the mechanical simulacrum of a human body. A pump to act as heart, oxygenators to act as lungs, thermostats, filters and a mass of complex chemical-balancing devices to ensure that the blood was kept in perfect condition.

Kill the body and the brain would die!

He started, shocked by the realisation that he was thinking of the machine as a human person, then became aware that someone was speaking to him.

'I beg your pardon?'

'Didn't you hear me?'

'No, I was thinking. What did you say?'

'Forget her,' said Jeff. He moved from the cabinet and Felix tensed before seeing that he was crossing the room towards Ottoway. 'Avril will keep. I was asking after the result of your studies.'

'I wasn't thinking about Avril,' said Felix. For some reason it was important to disassociate her from what he had to do. 'What was that about studies?'

'What's the matter with you?' Jeff frowned. 'You said that you had solved the cypher — the graphs. Well, what did you discover?'

'One thing,' said Felix evenly. 'Abic is insane!'

★ ★ ★

Ottoway grunted, the craggy mask of his face suddenly ugly with barely concealed anger.

'That,' he said acidly, 'is a damn stupid remark.'

'Thank you.'

'You asked for it, Felix.' Jeff obviously shared Ottoway's opinion.

'I don't think so.' Felix gestured towards the bulk of the artificial brain. 'What do you really know about this thing you've built? You took nucleic acids and stimulated them until they grew into a giant cortex. But what do you have?'

'A machine,' said Jeff quickly. 'An organic machine.'

'And what else is a man?'

'A man is the product of his environment,' said Ottoway. 'Are you trying to teach me basic physiology, Felix? To me a man is nothing but a collection of stimuli, a sensory recording device capable of

219

limited motion and restricted free will. He lives, moves and is governed by the world of his senses.'

'Exactly.' Ottoway, Felix saw, had expected opposition. 'I'm not arguing with you about that, Reg. I agree with you all the way.'

'So?'

'So take a new-born brain. Divorce it from all pre-conceived emotionally based external stimuli — isolate it from all humanity. Put it in a box and make certain that it lives and grows. What would we have then?'

'Abic isn't a human brain, Felix. The analogy isn't absolute.'

'I know that, but where is the difference? Abic is a cortex. It's capable of receiving and storing information. It contains an electric potential and that potential can be recorded on an encephalogram. It thinks, damn you! It thinks!'

They still wouldn't understand! Felix stared at them recognising their refusal to grasp the obvious and accept the inevitable. He swallowed, the gun a comforting bulk beneath his arm.

'By any standards you care to name,' he said quietly, 'Abic cannot be sane. It knows nothing of humanity, its very thought processes must move in alien channels, the world it has experienced is not the world as we know it. It is big and powerful. It could be malicious and I think it is. Or it could simply have the attributes of an accident prone in a magnified degree. That doesn't matter. The important thing is that it is dangerous and must be destroyed.'

He took the gun from beneath his coverall.

'You are going to destroy it!'

'You must be mad!' Ottoway stared at Felix with an incredulous expression. 'Felix! Is this your idea of a joke!'

'I'm not joking.' Felix lifted the gun. 'This insane thing is going to be destroyed.'

'You mean it!' Ottoway surged forward then halted as Jeff gripped his arm.

'Don't do it, Reg! That's Crombie's gun!'

'The Major — '

' — is perfectly all right.' Felix stepped

back from the machine resting his shoulders against the wall as he faced the two men. 'I don't want to kill you,' he said tightly, 'but this is too important to argue about. Jeff! Open that housing!'

'Go to hell!'

'Op . . . Ottoway! Don't . . . '

Felix ducked as Ottoway swung a heavy piece of apparatus from the bench poising it to throw into his face. Instinctively he squeezed the trigger, the bark of the gun loud in the confines of the laboratory. Metal shattered in Ottoway's hands and he slumped to the floor.

'You swine — '

Jeff came running, head low, hands outstretched in a flying tackle. Caught off balance Felix had no time to spring clear. Desperately he swung the gun, the heavy weapon smashing across Jeff's temple. Grimly he examined the two sprawled figures.

Jeff wasn't dead and neither, to his surprise, was Ottoway. The bullet had spent its force on the apparatus he had poised to throw, slamming it back in a knockout blow to the jaw. Both men would waken with headaches but that was all.

Relief was lost in the urgency of the moment. The shot would have been heard, he had to work fast.

Ducking under the rail Felix ran his hands over the metal housing. It was immobile, the dial of a combination lock a bland challenge which he found impossible to meet. Stepping back for fear of ricochets he aimed the pistol and pressed the trigger.

The hammer fell with a dry click.

Again he tried to fire, again, then frantically pressed the trigger with a succession of dry clicks as the gun stubbornly refused to fire. Breaking it he examined the cartridges. All bore the imprint of the firing pin. Only one had actually exploded.

Slamming the chamber back into position he aimed at the roof, squeezed the trigger, and swore as chips of stone fell from the roof. Again he tried to shoot off the lock and then gave up. There had to be another way.

A thin metal bar stood against one wall

and he gripped it, lifting it high before swinging it down towards the box with the full strength of his body.

The bar snapped as he began the downward swing.

It broke off a couple of inches from his hands, snapping as if made of fragile glass, the long, upper portion hurtling across the room to clatter harmlessly against a wall. Thrown off balance by the sudden lack of resistance Felix stumbled and fell heavily against the protective rail, half-stunned he staggered to his feet and flung the fragment of bar at the machine.

Conscious of the passing of time he stared wildly around the laboratory then snatched up a chair. It was made of a light alloy which yielded as he beat at the machine until it was a useless mass. Irritably he threw this aside, knowing that he was wasting precious time. He needed weight and mass if he hoped to shatter the box or penetrate the housing. That or explosives. The laboratory held neither.

Savagely he tugged at the protective rail then froze as the intercom burst into staccato life.

'Attention! Attention! Emergency call to all personnel. Felix Larsen must be apprehended on sight. Guards will go immediately to the bio-physical laboratory and protect Abic from wanton damage. Warning. Larsen is armed and dangerous. Take no chances!'

Time had run out!

17

He met the guard half-way down the passage leading from the laboratory. He fell without a sound as Crombie's pistol cracked against his jaw and Felix jumped over him, diving through the door just as a group of men came running down a passage.

'There he goes!'

'Halt or I fire!'

Lead whined from a wall as he ducked down a corridor, forgetting all caution in the burning need for speed. Twice he cannoned from the roof before adapting his stride. Behind him the shouts of the pursuers faded as he ran through the maze of passageways but he was not deluded into thinking that he had escaped.

He had to find somewhere to hide.

Not for long, that was impossible, but long enough to plan his next move. While he raced at random through the station he was only delaying his inevitable capture.

One of the safety doors blocked the passage and he ran towards it. It opened just as he reached it and he staggered back, blood coursing from his nose, his face a throbbing numbness from the impact with the metal panel. A man stood and gaped at him then slumped as Felix struck viciously at his head.

Where to hide?

A row of doors lined the wall and he tugged at one. It opened and he caught a glimpse of stacked crates. It was a storeroom and he ducked inside, slamming the door and leaning on it as the sound of running feet raced along outside. Sucking deep breaths he fought the desire to relax as he stared into the darkness. Then, careful to make no sound, he felt his way into the room and crouched behind a pile of boxes.

His face hurt and he touched it, feeling the warm wetness of blood and wondering if he had broken his nose. He wiped the blood on the sleeve of his coverall and cautiously touched the organ, wincing as bone grated beneath his fingers. But, broken or not, the nose was unimportant. He had more urgent things to do.

How to destroy Abic?

There were explosives in the arsenal but they would be guarded, especially now they were watching for him. Even if he could get explosives he would have to take them back into the laboratory and detonate them. The place was guarded now and it would be impossible to get back into the place. Jeff and Ottoway would see to that.

But if he couldn't get close to the thing how could he destroy it?

He crouched as the door swung open and light streamed in from the corridor outside. Two men, both alert, peered into the room. They had been well trained. While one looked the other stood ready, his rifle trained into the compartment. Had Felix been less cautious he would be dead or a prisoner by now.

'See anything?' The man with the rifle leaned forward a little.

'No.' His companion stepped into the room and slowly turned, his eyes gleaming in the reflected light as he searched the room.

'I knew he wouldn't be here,' said the man with the rifle. 'He probably ran straight on towards the living quarters. Come on, Harry, Echlan will be waiting for us at the hangar.'

The door swung shut and Felix relaxed his grip on the gun. He was trembling a little, a sure sign of nervous tension, but he forced himself to remain where he was. Running, no matter how strong the desire, was useless until he knew where he was going. Grimly he resumed his interrupted train of thought.

Explosives and direct attack were out. He could, he supposed, surrender to the Director and appeal to London but, while that would safeguard his person, it would not destroy the thing in the laboratory. Distance would weaken the urgency and no Government official would, on his own authority, order the destruction of expensive equipment. He would have to strike in some more subtle manner and he would have to do it quickly.

Softly Felix opened the door and stood listening through the gap. He waited until his ears told him that they had entered another room. Opening wide the door he stepped into the passage and ran towards the guards hoping to reach them before he was discovered. Luck was against him. The man with the rifle turned, his face startled over the barrel of his weapon as Felix lifted his pistol. Gunfire echoed from the walls.

Something hit Felix's pistol, the bullet from the guard's rifle knocking the weapon up and to one side as he pressed the trigger. Lead screamed from a wall in a wild ricochet and smashed the rifle from the guard's hands. Foolishly he stared at it then Felix was on him, his weighted hand cracking at his jaw, his other hand snatching up the fallen weapon.

Frantically he raced down the passage away from the shouts of the other guard.

There was only one way he could go — only one thing he could do. Abic depended on an electrically powered pump and, if the power to that pump could be cut, the artificial brain would die.

★　★　★

The passage opened on a wide area which seemed filled with people. He thrust through them, the blood-stained coverall, his weapons, the battered mask of his face attracting immediate attention.

'Felix!'

He raced past a man and shouldered another aside before running down a corridor. He had taken the wrong passage and he cursed as he found himself facing a knot of guards. Echlan was among them.

'Felix! Stop you fool!'

'Stand back!'

The rifle kicked in his hands and lead whined from the ceiling.

'I mean it, Echlan! Stand back all of you!'

They obeyed, turning as he ordered, faces to the wall, hands resting above their heads. Echlan stared over his shoulder as Felix approached.

'You can't get away, man! Keep this up

and you'll be shot.'

'I don't think so.' Staring at the sergeant Felix had an idea. He thrust the pistol beneath his belt and jammed the muzzle of the rifle into the other's spine. 'All right, Echlan, you lead the way. I want to get to the power plant, you know where it is.'

Echlan didn't move.

'You heard me!' Felix twisted the butt, grinding the barrel into the other's back. 'You're going to be my hostage.' He shouted at the others. 'You hear that? If I'm attacked Echlan dies!' He twisted the butt again. 'Right! Now move!'

'You're mad,' said Echlan, but he began to walk down the passage. 'You're clean off your rocker.'

'Shut up and keep walking.'

'What's it all for, Felix? What do you hope to gain?'

'I know what I'm doing!'

'Sure, you want to destroy Abic, but why?'

'The thing's insane. I . . . ' Felix broke off. 'How did you know what I wanted?'

'Crombie told us. He was found by the

guard shortly after you left and gave the warning when he recovered.' Echlan stared over his shoulder. 'You're sick, Felix. Why don't you just call the whole thing off?'

'Keep walking!'

Felix was puzzled. Crombie had been drugged and, even if the guard had found him, still the drug would have taken time to work itself harmless. Echlan answered his unspoken questions.

'Sir Ian came when the guard called in,' he said. 'He pumped the Major out and gave him something to pull him round. He alerted the station as soon as he recovered.'

'I see.'

Felix was thoughtful. It accounted for his failure to recognise the warning voice but it told him more than that. Crombie had acted too precipitately. He could have sent guards to the laboratory and Felix would have been trapped without a chance to escape. Instead he had issued a general warning. Only his desperate fear for the safety of the brain could have prompted that.

The brain! The damn thing which squatted like a spider in the station spinning its invisible web of mental force. An idiot intelligence which caused accidents, destroyed men and machines and, because of its insanity, had somehow contaminated the entire personnel of the station.

For madness was contagious, Felix knew that from experience. Abnormal behaviour tends to become the norm and, given a giant cortex with magnified mental emissions how could those around it have retained their sanity? It was the answer to all the oddities he had noticed, the slackening of discipline, the accepted customs which, when viewed coldly, were inexplicable to the people who composed the personnel. They themselves might not know how they had altered but he did.

He tried to win Echlan over.

'Listen,' he said urgently. 'You are a thinking man. What would you do if something threatened the station?'

'Fight it.'

'Right, that's what I'm trying to do. Why don't you help me?'

'You must be joking.' Echlan looked over his shoulder. 'If you ask me that accident you had has affected your brain. What's in the station that's so bad?'

Felix told him. Echlan laughed.

'You don't believe me?'

'How can I? What harm can a thing in a box do?'

'If it were a bomb in a box you'd think differently,' snapped Felix. His voice was sharp with desperation. 'Well, Abic is worse than any bomb. I honestly believe that it has altered the personalities of those in this station. Crombie, Ottoway, Jeff, maybe others.'

'Sir Ian?'

Felix hesitated. He was thinking of the magnetic-accelerator and its potential. Why should Macdonald have even thought of its construction? And the Eyrie, what explanation could he have for that other than what Felix suspected?

'Well?' Echlan's voice was a caustic rasp. 'Is the Director one of your bogey man's victims?'

'I don't know.'

It would be useless to offend the

sergeant. Echlan, obviously, had the highest regard for Macdonald and would hear nothing against him. Felix had a flicker of hope. If he could persuade the man that Sir Ian was threatened he might yet win his support.

'Look at it . . . '

He stumbled, his ankle twisting beneath his weight and the rifle fell from Echlan's spine. He sprang forward towards a branching corridor and ducked into it as Felix recovered. His voice echoed from the tunnel.

'You can't win, Felix. Give up now before you get hurt!'

Then he was gone, the sound of his running feet echoing from the passage.

★   ★   ★

Felix ran after him, caught a glimpse of a closing door and dived through it just in time to see Echlan vanish from the end of the tunnel. By the time he reached the end the area was deserted. He started down a passage, heard the sound of voices from the far end and doubled back. The intercom broke into life.

'Attention all personnel. Go to your quarters and remain. Guards in sector eight will move forward and bar passages seventeen to twenty-two. Guards in sector five will withdraw to sector six.'

Passages seventeen to twenty-two were those leading towards the power plant. Echlan had reported and Crombie was sealing the area.

It was now impossible to cut off the power.

Felix ran down a corridor, cursing the lack of directions and the similarity of the tunnels but knowing that he had to keep moving. A shout echoed behind him as he passed a junction and he ran frantically from the chasing guards. A wide area opened before him and he ran across it, dived down a tunnel chosen at random and lunged through a safety door. Twenty more paces and he recognised where he was.

He fought the instinct to run to his own quarters. There was no help for him there.

'Felix!' The intercom filled the station

with its mechanical voice. 'Crombie speaking. Give up before you get hurt.'

'Go to hell!'

Felix glared at the black box and resisted the temptation to thumb the button and yell defiance. If he did then control would have him located.

'Felix, you don't understand.' That was Avril's voice. 'Please give yourself up. Please!'

He ran from the voice knowing that he couldn't escape it but running just the same. He was a rabbit running wildly in a warren with the ferrets of guards coming closer all the time. They were in no hurry. He could do no damage. His capture was simply a matter of time.

'Felix!'

Echlan ran towards him, armed guards at his back. Felix fired, the bullet whining from the roof then ran back down the corridor, his back cringing to the impact of expected lead. The guards didn't fire and he reached the end of the passage, ran down a wider tunnel and reached an unfinished corridor. He ran down it, pressing past a heap of broken stone and halting as he reached the far side of a chamber.

Bleakly he stared at the dead end of the rock face.

'He ran down there, Sarge.'

Voices echoed down the tunnel followed by the cautious shuffle of feet.

'Watch it, Sam. He's armed and there's too much cover for my liking.'

'He's too quick on the trigger.'

'I don't know. He aimed high, remember.'

'Shut up!' Echlan's voice rose above the babble. 'We know you're in there, Felix, and you can't get out. Throw out your guns and come out with your hands over your head.'

Felix didn't answer. He crouched behind the edge of the tunnel and looked down it to where the men were standing. He couldn't see them but, if they tried to approach, they would have to pass the heap of broken stone. Carefully he sighted the rifle.

'Echlan!' His voice followed the crashing echoes of the shot. 'Echlan! Can you hear me?'

'Yes.'

'Listen! If any of you try to come in here I'll shoot to kill.'

'What good will that do?' The sergeant spoke with quiet reasonableness. 'We'll get you in the end. Why don't you just give up?'

'I will — as soon as Sir Ian gets here.'

'But — '

'You heard what I said!' Felix sent another bullet into the heap of stone. 'I mean it, Echlan. Get the Director here and I'll give up.'

It was the only thing he could do. Sir Ian might be contaminated by Abic's insanity but he was still the Director and a responsible person. And there was always the chance that he didn't know. Crombie could have told him that Felix was an enemy agent, anything to account for his actions. Perhaps he, like Echlan, thought that Felix was suffering from the delayed effects of his accident. But he would know the truth, Felix would see to that.

'Felix.'

He looked up, aware that he had

relaxed his vigilance, then eased his finger from the trigger as he recognised the man standing by the heap of stone.

'Felix?' Macdonald took another step forward. 'Where are you?'

'Here.' Felix rose. 'I'm sorry about this, Sir Ian, but there's something you've got to know.'

He told the Director what he had learned. Macdonald listened with quiet courtesy then held out his hand.

'Give me your guns, Felix.'

'What are you going to do, Sir Ian?'

'First I think you need a wash and then something for that face of yours. It must be quite painful. The guns, please.'

'But Abic? You will destroy it?'

'Shall we discuss that later?' Macdonald was very close. Felix didn't resist as he took the pistol and rifle.

It was good to relinquish responsibility. Good to be able to relax and leave the necessity of making decisions to someone else. He had tried and he had failed now it was up to the Director.

Felix recognised the withdrawal symptoms and knew they were wrong. A man couldn't run and yield and leave it to others. That was the trouble with the world, too many people were content to leave the very survival of the race to those few who were not retrogressive. It was wrong to ignore the primitive aggressions.

Wrong, and dangerous. Felix knew it as he stepped into the corridor among Echlan and his men. For Macdonald had not been shocked, nor been incredulous. He had displayed none of the reactions Felix had expected and that could mean only one thing.

Nothing he had heard had come as a surprise.

18

They had been very kind. Felix had bathed and changed and Gloria had fixed his face. Now they sat in the Eyrie, the room with the window and the wonderful view. It surprised Felix a little. He was, by the standards of the station, a criminal and had expected to be treated as such. This generosity made him cautious.

'I think you should know,' he said, 'that I am the direct representative of Sir Joshua Aarons.'

'I know.'

'You know?' Macdonald's answer startled Felix. Then he guessed. 'I see. Gloria?'

'No, you weren't subjected to hypnosis or drugs if that is what you think. But it was obvious that you were other than what you appeared to be. While you lay unconscious after your accident we were sure of it. You rambled a little. It was a tremendous shock, after all.'

'Yes.' Felix looked at his hands. 'I would

like to contact Sir Joshua. I can give your operator the code signal.'

'I know Sir Joshua,' said Macdonald. 'A fine man.'

'Are you going to let me talk to him?'

'Certainly. Did you have any doubt?'

There was a catch, Felix was sure of it. The Director couldn't simply let him talk to the head of security and tell him the truth about the station. No man willingly commits political suicide. Macdonald must have guessed his thoughts.

'We aren't savages here, Felix. What else can we do but permit you to talk with your superior?'

'You could kill me.'

Macdonald smiled and shook his head.

'No,' he said gently. 'That is the one thing we cannot do. We can't kill you any more than you could kill one of us. No one can die that way here in the station.'

It took seconds for the full implication of Macdonald's remark to register.

'That's impossible!' Felix surged to his feet and took three steps towards the window. He turned and stared at the calm, bland faces. 'That's impossible!' he repeated.

'No. Think about it for a moment.'

★   ★   ★

He had the clues, all of them, and if he had a brain and imagination at all he should be able to find the answer. Not a different man, perhaps, but he was a trained psychologist able to probe actions and find motivations, delving beneath the surface to discover unsuspected truth. There was a wrongness about the station due, he'd guessed, to the presence of the artificial brain. But, ignoring the doubtful question of actual mental possession, just what constituted that stable air of wrongness?

He thought about it, sitting chin on hand, elbow on knee, eyes shadowed as he consciously dismissed all illogical, emotion-based reactions to unfamiliar elements, concentrating instead on observed phenomena.

The total absence of strain and tension within the station. The calm acceptance that even would-be suicides could be trusted to continue their duties without fear of harm. The homogeneousness of the personnel almost as if they were one big family.

Family!

The Father Image!

The station considered itself to be under some benevolent protection!

But why? How?

Then, suddenly, the pieces fitted and he knew.

★   ★   ★

'The accidents,' he said. 'There are too many coincidences.'

'Yes.' Macdonald sighed as if with relief. 'Now you know what Abic does.'

Felix nodded. Now it all seemed so obvious. It had been, as Gloria had said, a matter of looking at the data from a different point of view.

'There are accident prones,' said Macdonald, 'and there is luck and we have known of the latter since the dawn of Mankind. Always there have been

246

those with charmed lives and there have been the reverse too. So luck, good or bad, must be an actual force, a natural force similar to gravitation or magnetism or even electricity. A force as universal as those we know but on a different plane. It exists, we are surrounded by its effects, but only now can we begin to appreciate how it works.'

'Why aren't all accidents the same? A man can fall a foot and break his neck, another sixty feet and walk away unbruised. A man can try to shoot himself and the cartridge will misfire, another will die from the prick of a pin. Gamblers rely on luck, the probabilities of odds being in their favour and they can develop a skill in which they seem to control the very random factors of chance — if they are as random as we have always believed.'

'Are they random?'

'I think they are, as magnetism is or electricity, but we can harness those forces and we have, in a way, harnessed the forces which we call luck.' Macdonald smiled. 'Or rather Abic has done it for us.'

It fitted! It fitted in a way which Felix found almost frightening.

'I believe that only a human brain can control this force,' continued Macdonald. 'We have all experienced luck both good and bad, and we all know of particularly 'lucky' or 'unlucky' types. Abic is the largest cortex known. It is, in almost every way, a facsimile of a human brain. It seems only reasonable to assume that, whatever powers we possess, it possesses them also but to a greater degree. Ottoway says, and I agree with him, that our own power is latent, buried in the parts of the brain for which we seem to have no use. Abic's is far from latent.'

'But it is locked in a box, deaf, blind, unaware . . . ' Felix's voice trailed into silence as he saw his error. Abic was connected to the electrical system of the station and its 'senses' must follow every wire. The intercom boxes alone would relay every scrap of information within the station to the artificial brain and God alone knew what other senses it had been forced to develop. It could probably 'see' magnetism, gravitation, the pulse of electrons and the entire electromagnetic spectrum.

He had underestimated the brain.

'Gloria says that a lucky accident is a combination of fortuitous circumstances, Sir Ian,' he said. Macdonald nodded his head, as he stood by her chair, gently stroking her hair.

'She spotted the unusual circumstances of our accidents almost right away,' he said. 'Routine checking connected them with Abic, exactly as you yourself found the relationship. We were,' his smile broadened a little, 'less precipitate shall we say?'

'No, Sir Ian. You were more scientific. Do you know just how this — power — operates?'

'Not exactly, but we can make a reasonable assumption. It is a matter of selecting probabilities. For example, when you aim a pistol and pull the trigger two things can happen. The cartridge will or will not fire. If it does fire then again there is a choice. The bullet may or may not hit the target. If it does hit the target it may or may not strike a vital organ and so on. Luck, good luck, is a matter of selecting and combining positive — beneficial — probabilities. We all, in some degree, have that power. If we are exceptionally good at it then we have a 'charmed life'. Few people, unfortunately, are that good.'

It was a facile explanation but there were flaws. Felix could admit that it covered everything which had disturbed him but even so something remained.

'What about Leaver? He died from a minor fall.'

'Leaver was an enemy agent. We found a micro-radio when we examined his body. We had picked up odd transmissions and suspected him.' Macdonald glanced at Avril. 'He deserved to die.'

'But — '

'An organism has the right to defend itself,' said Gloria gently. It was answer enough.

'But the Commission?' Felix waved her to silence. 'Never mind. I can guess. They must have talked and decided to replace the executive staff of the station and garrisoning it with American personnel.

Abic would consider that to be a threat. Rockets are delicate things and it would be simple to ensure that an essential part malfunctioned at a critical moment.' He gave a shaky laugh. 'How does it feel to be the protected children of a devoted father?'

He hadn't expected an answer.

'But there's one thing which doesn't fit,' he said bitterly. 'I tried to kill Abic. Why didn't it eliminate me?'

'Because it couldn't,' said Gloria. 'Because, within you, is a part of itself!'

Father fighting son. It seemed incredible and yet — father fighting son!

'You know what we do here,' said Macdonald grimly. 'We search for better ways to eliminate the human race. Well, we found the ultimate in horror, but even our politicians are not yet so insane that they want to commit suicide. So we looked for something to defeat what we had found. You know about nerve gases?'

Felix nodded.

'Our virus is based on the action of those gases and there can be no defence. So we built the brain to help us find an answer. We wanted something, anything, to save the race from its own madness. Telling them isn't enough. People refuse to believe in annihilation.'

'Naturally.' Felix stared at the Director. 'Does that surprise you? Everyone lives with the knowledge of his own death. Telling him it may be a little closer or more widespread doesn't make it any more dreadful. To any thinking being personal death is the most dreadful thing there can be. If he can live with that knowledge how can you hope to frighten him with anything else?'

'But no one admits, consciously at least, that he is going to die,' said Gloria.

'Agreed. But he knows that he is living a lie and still he manages to ignore it. Against that armour you don't stand a chance. Personal death is, after all, a certainty. The ultimate war is only a probability.'

Felix looked back at the Director.

'You were saying, Sir Ian?'

'We built the brain,' continued Macdonald evenly. 'Then Seldon had his accident. In order to save his life we had to attach him to a blood supply. We had to work fast and the only blood we had available was that used by Abic. It worked.'

'I see.' Felix was beginning to understand. The same blood which had passed through the artificial brain had been introduced to Seldon. The same blood!

'Seldon became — contaminated.' Gloria looked steadily at Felix. 'The blood contained a virus which acts like a symbiote and lodges in the brain. It spread throughout the station.'

She would have been the first, of course, tending Seldon as she did. His breath would have carried it, riding on the air pumped past his larynx if in no other way. She would have spread it in turn, he remembered the carved bust and the way Macdonald had stroked her hair. They were both human. Perhaps too human. Any contact disease would propagate swiftly in the station. He remembered Avril's first kiss.

'My illness — ?'

'Yes. You, like the rest of us, are protected against mischance. You cannot be killed in accidents which would kill other men. If anyone tries to shoot you the gun will misfire or the bullet miss.'

Felix touched his face.

'That was the most Abic could do,' she said. 'It was, after all, trying to protect itself.'

'The Commission . . . ?' He let his voice trail into silence. He knew the answer to that one. No one would have kissed the members of the Commission.

But still there were questions.

'The virus? Can it be controlled?'

'That isn't the difficulty.' Macdonald sounded tired. 'Why are the destructive things of life always the most prolific? Weeds among crops. Malignant bacteria instead of beneficient? Parasites instead of helpful symbiotes. The hope of the world lies in that virus but, as yet, we cannot develop it to the point where it can be of any real use.'

'Develop it?'

'Yes. The entire resources of the station are concentrated on that aim. We need to make it as prolific and as hardy as the nerve virus is deadly.'

'Are you insane?' Felix could hardly believe what he was hearing. 'Do you intend to spread the disease over Earth?'

He remembered the magnetic accelerator and had his answer.

'You traitor!'

'Fool!'

For the first time he saw Macdonald in anger and it was something he would never forget. It was a cold, consuming rage which filled the man and turned him from a pleasant man of title into a ruthless animal of concentrated purpose. But the anger wasn't for Felix, he was too small for such a rage. It was fury at the stupidity of the world.

'Look at it!' Macdonald gestured towards the window beyond which hung the ball of the earth. 'Beautiful, isn't it! We should revere it but instead we are trying to destroy it. And we can destroy it never doubt that. With bombs and microbes we can turn that world into a barren ball of dust. Am I a traitor for trying to prevent that?'

'I . . .'

'What are petty loyalties in such a

case?' Macdonald drew a deep breath. 'I am no traitor. If Britain can save the world from destruction then she will have cause to be proud. But even if I have to defy my country I will do what has to be done. There is only one real loyalty — loyalty to the human race. Fools must not be permitted to destroy it.'

'How can you stop them?' Felix felt some of Macdonald's anger. 'By threatening the world with your microbes?'

'If necessary, yes!'

'They will annihilate you. All the nations will unite to wipe you out.'

'Perhaps, but I doubt it. Unity demands mutual trust and that is something which it is safe to assume will not exist. But it will, I hope, never come to that. All we need is time in order to develop the one thing which will make the world safe forever.'

Macdonald grew suddenly calm and Felix revised his previous hasty opinion. Macdonald wasn't a fanatic. Nor was he insane. He was simply a dedicated man. There was a world of difference.

★ ★ ★

He was right, of course, there was no doubt about that. If the virus could be developed and spread over the planet then global war would be a nightmare of the past. In fact any sort of war would be impossible. With the probability factor working to save each man from harm how could guns fire, bombs explode, bacteria be released?

For a moment Felix sat in a dream world of imagination. He started as Avril touched his hand.

'Well, Felix?'

'Well, what?' He was confused. They were all, he noticed, watching him. He felt very small as he realised why.

'I thought I was investigating you,' he said. 'I imagined that I was being clever but, all the time, it was you who were investigating me. Was the experiment a success?'

'It was necessary, Felix,' said Gloria. She did not apologise. 'We had discussed what was best to do. Some thought that if our discovery was announced to selected scientists we would gain their co-operation. Others doubted that. Then you arrived and offered us the chance to conduct a controlled experiment. It was — interesting.'

'I can imagine,' said Felix drily. She shook her head.

'No, Felix, we weren't making sport of you. We couldn't be certain that the virus had bred true or even that it was still active once assimilated. You proved that it had and that it was. Now all we need is time.'

'You'll have your time,' he said, and suddenly made his decision. 'With luck on our side how can we lose?'

'We?' He saw the hope in her eyes, in all their eyes.

'Yes.' He rose and felt Avril's hand slip within his own. 'Sir Joshua is waiting for my report. It will be favourable but I will tell him I should remain. He will agree — with Seldon of no further use he will have little choice. Together we'll get the world out of its mess.' He squeezed Avril's hand.

'Felix!' She looked at him, her eyes

bright. They grew brighter as he said the three words she had waited to hear. It was natural for them to kiss.

'One last question, Sir Ian.' Felix stood, his arm around Avril's waist. 'Why did you build this room and this window?'

'To remind us of our humanity,' said Macdonald softly, he was looking at the earth.

'Just in case we should ever be tempted to forget.'

THE END

We do hope that you have enjoyed reading this large print book.

Did you know that all of our titles are available for purchase?

We publish a wide range of high quality large print books including:
Romances, Mysteries, Classics
General Fiction
Non Fiction and Westerns

Special interest titles available in large print are:
The Little Oxford Dictionary
Music Book, Song Book
Hymn Book, Service Book

Also available from us courtesy of Oxford University Press:
Young Readers' Dictionary
(large print edition)
Young Readers' Thesaurus
(large print edition)

For further information or a free brochure, please contact us at:
Ulverscroft Large Print Books Ltd.,
The Green, Bradgate Road, Anstey,
Leicester, LE7 7FU, England.
Tel: (00 44) **0116 236 4325**
Fax: (00 44) **0116 234 0205**

Other titles in the
Linford Mystery Library:

A TIME FOR MURDER

John Glasby

Carlos Galecci, a top man in organized crime, has been murdered — and the manner of his death is extraordinary . . . He'd last been seen the previous night, entering his private vault, to which only he knew the combination. When he fails to emerge by the next morning, his staff have the metal door cut open — to discover Galecci dead with a knife in his back. Private detective Johnny Merak is hired to find the murderer and discover how the impossible crime was committed — but is soon under threat of death himself . . .

CRYPTIC CLUE

Peter Conway

Fiona Graham, a physiotherapist, is found naked and lying face down in the swimming pool of Croxley Hall health farm where she worked. The coroner's verdict: accidental death by drowning. However, both her father and Golding, the forensic pathologist, disagree with his ruling. Inspector Roger Newton arrives with his assistant, Jane Warwick, to investigate a murder. But when Jane disappears, it's a race to unravel the 'Cryptic Clue' to her whereabouts — and the reason for Fiona's death.

THE BLACK CANDLE

Evelyn Harris

With Chatton Eastwood's history of Satan worship, the locals believed that black magic was again rife. And witchcraft became a cover for premeditated murder. Children, playing in a quarry, found the body later identified as Amos White, missing since the theft of two priceless tapestries. But the real Amos was secretly buried in Drearden's Wood. His killer knew it — so did the blackmailer — as well as some inconvenient facts about a lot of people . . . And death could not fail to come again.

BOOGIE WAS A GENT

Philip Lauben

Harold Boomgard had seemed a meek little man, working for a respectable company. So when he dies after collapsing in the washroom of a snackbar, there is nothing immediately suspicious about it. But his wife is certain her husband had never owned that flashy tie or dreadful hat . . . Investigating, Captain Homer Clay of Homicide finds that Harold's firm had closed almost a year ago — yet his income had risen considerably. As Clay uncovers Harold's activities, he also turns up more surprises.

BLOOD ON THE ROCKS

Archie Venters

The ground beneath Kennedy rolled like an ocean swell with flame blazing from the tower's arrow slits and roof. At the peak a tiny figure hovered and plunged downwards ... The tough Glasgow journalist was hitting back — his trail of vengeance blasting a sleepy Scottish island wide open. As gunfire shatters the peace, he fights like a cornered rat. Then, joined by a group of ordinary islanders, Kennedy faces a final fatal battle with a gang of desperate killers.

THE MASTER MUST DIE

John Russell Fearn

Gyron de London, a powerful industrialist of the year 2190, receives a letter warning him of his doom on the 30th March, three weeks hence. Despite his precautions — being sealed in a guarded, radiation-proof cube — he dies on the specified day, as forecast! When scientific investigator Adam Quirke is called to investigate, he discovers that de London had been the victim of a highly scientific murder — but who was the murderer, and how was this apparently impossible crime committed?